My Contract
with Henry

My Contract with Henry

ROBIN VAUPEL

Holiday House / New York

Library of Congress Cataloging-in-Publication Data
Vaupel, Robin.
My contract with Henry / by Robin Vaupel.
p.   cm.
Summary: A mission that begins as an eighth-grade project on Henry David Thoreau's
experimental living at Walden Pond becomes a life-changing experience for a group of outsider
students who become budding philosophers, environmental activists, and loyal friends.
ISBN 0-8234-1701-8 (hardcover)
1. Thoreau, Henry David, 1817–1862. Walden—Juvenile fiction. [1. Thoreau, Henry David,
1817–1862. Walden—Fiction.   2. Friendship—Fiction.   3. Schools—Fiction.]   I. Title.
PZ7.V468 My 2003

[Fic]—dc21   2002027471

For Mother

My Contract with Henry

Chapter 1

"How could youths better learn to live than by at
once trying the experiment of living?"
H. D. THOREAU

Mrs. Stark's classroom was an unlikely place to meet a rebel. So when we opened our literature books to a new chapter on Monday, I was shocked to see a person who actually looked interesting. Henry David Thoreau was standing at the bottom of the page in a straw hat that covered most of his rumpled hair and an old-fashioned coat. A squirrel was sitting on his shoe, its tail curled around his ankle. I liked Henry right off. In fact, I liked him even before the riffling of pages stopped and the other kids in my ninth-grade English class landed on the page with me.

"Class, you are about to meet one of the most important authors of the nineteenth century, Mr. Henry David Thoreau."

Mrs. Stark paused to let this proclamation sink in, but I was way ahead of her.

I'd already skimmed enough to realize that this was not your typical dead writer. Scattered throughout the chapter were sketches of forests, lakes, insects, and woodchucks. There was even a picture of the jail cell where Henry spent the night to protest slavery. While Mrs. Stark pulled down a map and put some dates on the board, I leafed through the chapter and made another discovery. Henry David Thoreau, with his serious, deep-set eyes, was going to rescue me from my life.

Mrs. Stark picked students randomly to read Henry's essay. I settled back and relaxed. My name, Gardner, Beth, put me in the middle of Mrs. Stark's alphabetized seating chart, in a sort of no-man's-land, behind a large boy named Brendan Fain. I'd been doing my best to disappear since my first day at Pine Brook School, so my seat suited me fine. Even Mrs. Stark missed me when she scanned her list and went looking for oral readers. Henry said, "I never found the companion that was so companionable as solitude." I knew what he meant, because that pretty much summed up my school year so far.

Henry had written a book called *Walden,* and our text had a few chapters from it. He'd built a tiny cabin on a hill overlooking Walden Pond in Concord, Massachusetts. For more than two years, he'd lived there alone, studying the pond and the surrounding forests, keeping a journal, and living as simply as he could. He thought the people in town were perfect fools for living in big fancy houses and owning more junk than they knew what to do with. The problem with owning lots of things, he said, was that the things actually owned us. According to Henry, we were all prisoners, slaving our lives away to pay for our useless stuff.

"Here we have one of Mr. Thoreau's most famous quotes," Mrs. Stark said, pointing to the chalkboard. "Who would like to read it for us?" Her squinty eyes flashed beneath her black bangs. Several hands went up, but she studied her seating chart and chose Janice Phelson.

"I went to the woods because I wished to live deliberately, to front only the essential facts of life, and see if I could not learn what it had to teach, and not, when I came to die, discover that I had not lived."

One of the nice things about invisibility is the freedom it gives you in class. I looked around to see what effect Henry was having on my classmates. Kathy Dulack examined her split ends with great interest. Larry Duncan drummed his fingers on the book and waited for the minute hand to creep around the clock. Ben Jones angled his foot back to admire his new tennis shoe. No one was listening to Henry; they hadn't even heard his knock at the door. But I had.

What I couldn't get over was how much Henry and I had in common. True, he was living in Massachusetts and the year was 1845, but Michigan wasn't too far off, and a century

3

and a half isn't that long. He'd lost his brother John to lock-jaw, and I'd lost my father to a heart attack some years before. And his little cabin on Walden Pond reminded me of the clapboard cottage where I lived with my mother, though ours wasn't nearly as cozy as his. Henry had left the comfort of the town and so had we, though Mother and I had moved because we had no other choice. My father's death had left us without savings and without an income, so we'd sold our Meadow-creek Hills home and rented a small run-down house across town. Here was one huge difference though: Henry kept his cabin simple and bare so that the forest could seep in through the door and window, but not us. Our house was packed with my mother's velour couches, her antique tables, her heirloom china. She could have been lighthearted about our simple life, like Henry was, but instead she clung to her sterling silver and crystal as if they were life rafts.

Henry and I were both alone a lot. Mother worked as a receptionist in a real estate firm and often had to work late. I usually cooked dinner and then did my homework, waiting for her headlights to sweep across the house as she turned in the drive. Sitting there night after night in the yellow light of our kitchen, without a soul to talk to, it's no wonder I was ready for Henry David Thoreau.

It took us about a week to finish *Walden*. My classmates were totally bored. To them Henry was just another dull chapter inside an even duller unit called "Voices of the Nineteenth Century." But I was so charged by Henry's life that sometimes I had to sit on my hands to keep from applauding.

4

If I wasn't careful, someone was going to notice the invisible girl in Seat 5 Row 4.

Henry had plenty of critics in Mrs. Stark's class, and they weren't sitting on their hands. Ben Jones and Larry Duncan, two good-looking athletes, became the loudest spokesmen for the anti-Henry faction. To hear this Thoreau, this madman, say he liked being alone was weird, to spend all day enjoying nature was even weirder, but this business of "simplicity, simplicity" was taking it too far.

"What's wrong with having a big house and a good job and going on vacations?" Larry wanted to know. "My dad likes being a lawyer, and he takes us to Florida every year."

"Perhaps the difference can be explained this way," Mrs. Stark said mysteriously. "Mr. Thoreau was a *transcendentalist*."

"A what?" Larry smirked and glanced back at his buddy Ben and a grinning blond boy named Chip Harris. They all sneered at the strange word. I didn't understand it any more than they did, but I liked the sound of it.

"To *transcend* means to rise above," Mrs. Stark explained. "Mr. Thoreau and his friends were seeking a higher reality beyond this material world."

I sat up, electrified. That was exactly what I wanted to do! When your present reality is a crowded school where no one calls to you in the mornings as you get off the bus or pulls you into the lunch line or waits by your locker, then, naturally, you start thinking about other realities, better ones.

Larry, however, wasn't as inspired by transcendentalism. "Yeah, well I'd hate it if my dad sat around watching the birds all day like this guy."

Most of the class agreed with Larry. They wanted more, not less. Mrs. Stark's room became chaotic. Kids were talking out of turn, calling out insults to Henry, making bird sounds. Suddenly Mrs. Stark slapped her hands together, and it felt as though a shaft of lightning had split her room.

"That will be enough!" she snapped. "I think we should test Mr. Thoreau's ideas before we dismiss them so easily. Mr. Thoreau's years at Walden Pond have been called an 'experiment in essential living.' Perhaps we should experiment a bit ourselves."

Ben Jones jumped in. "How can we do that? This Walden thing was like, way long ago."

Mrs. Stark wheeled on him as if she'd been hoping someone might say that. "Are you suggesting, Mr. Jones, that the concept of simple living has no relevancy to our modern life?"

Clearly, Ben had leaped in over his head. "I'm . . . n-not sure," he stammered.

"Precisely!" Mrs. Stark said, pointing to the board again. "Which is why I am suggesting that we all go to the woods and live deliberately. Let's 'front only the essential facts of life' and see if we cannot learn what they have to teach."

Marjorie Winfred, a pale, freckled, timid girl, asked in amazement, "Are we going on a field trip, Mrs. Stark?"

"No, no. I want each of you to select some portion of

6

Mr. Thoreau's philosophy and put it into practice." Mrs. Stark hesitated; the assignment seemed to be coming to her in fragments. We watched her nervously, for nothing is worse than assignments that teachers make up in the heat of the moment. "Let's see. . . . You'll work with a small group and develop a . . . project, yes, something that reflects your Walden experience. We'll call it our Experiment in Living, and it will comprise your final grade for the unit. Tomorrow you'll select your partners and begin this exciting adventure."

Janice Phelson had her planning calendar out. "When will it be due, Mrs. Stark?"

"Oh—well, let me think. The results of your experiments will be due . . . the week before Thanksgiving. That will afford you plenty of time to immerse yourselves in the mind of Mr. Thoreau."

There was a collective gasp. "You mean we have to pretend to be this guy for six weeks?" Chip asked.

Now that she'd figured out all the details, Mrs. Stark sounded confident again. "If Mr. Thoreau could spend two years examining his life, I think we can spare less than two months, Mr. Harris. And please know that I am expecting products of real substance, evidence that your lives have been touched by this experience." The bell rang, and before anyone else could object, Mrs. Stark crinkled her face into a smile and dismissed us.

I didn't think about the Experiment in Living until later that night. When I got home, I scrounged in the pantry and made macaroni and cheese, reading the recipe variations on the box as I ate. Later I turned on the TV and let it run unwatched in the living room. I did my homework on my bed, finishing up with my literature book and reading again Henry's story of his life in the woods.

I wanted to crawl inside those chapters and live at Walden Pond. I'd been seeing myself tagging along with Henry on hikes, following this man who saw more in one square foot of forest than most people saw in their lifetimes. But suddenly Walden Pond didn't seem as private anymore, now that Mrs. Stark had invited the whole class out there. Tomorrow loomed blacker than the panes of my bedroom window. Mrs. Stark's "exciting adventure" would mean experimenting with a bunch of kids I didn't know. Even worse, it would mean becoming visible.

Chapter 2

"We are for the most part more lonely when
we go abroad among men than when
we stay in our chambers."
H. D. THOREAU

The next day the scene in Mrs. Stark's room overwhelmed me. I had expected an unusual day, an uncomfortable day, but I wasn't prepared for the all-out savagery of Pick Your Partners Day. The confusion began when we walked in and found our neat, dependable rows gone. The desks had been clustered into little groups, and Mrs. Stark was flitting around like a nervous hostess.

"Well, come along then." She waved us into the room. "Find your partners and let the Experiment begin!"

For those with friends in English class, it must have been fun lunging for seats, shifting, negotiating to find the perfect group. For those of us who were unknown and unclaimed, it was a long five minutes. We wandered around untouched through the frenzy until finally we drifted like survivors of a plane crash toward the only empty cluster of desks.

There was squealing and laughter all around us, but in my group we looked one another over in numb silence. Beside me was Hollis Robbins. He was skinny and disheveled and looked to be about nine years old. On my other side sat Rachel Haygen, a heavy girl with long, messy hair. She shoved her glasses against the bridge of her nose and retreated even further into the novel she had flattened against her books. I'd never noticed either of them. Like me, they had been yanked out of their hiding places and thrust into the visible world.

And sitting across from me was Stuart Garfield, a boy who could never be invisible. For one thing, he was the tallest student at Pine Brook School. Square-jawed, clear-eyed, Stuart had the beginnings of a handsome face, but you had to be perceptive. To appreciate Stuart's potential, you had to see about ten years into the future, when all the construction would finally be finished. But right now the most startling thing about Stuart wasn't his looks. What made him unique was his enthusiasm. It radiated out of him like sunlight. Even now, sitting with three social rejects, he looked very pleased and already very busy.

He pointed his pencil at us in turn. "Let's see if I've got this right. Hollis Robbins, Beth Gardner, and . . ."—he jotted down a few more notes—"you're Rachel Haygen."

Rachel didn't even glance up from her book.

He slid his pencil behind his ear. "I'm Stuart Garfield, and I must say that I couldn't have handpicked a better group. I mean, we've definitely got the best chance of making the experiment a success."

Hollis nodded uncertainly and I tried to smile. Rachel ignored us all.

"Well, it seems that we agree on that point," Stuart said after a polite pause. "So what do you think we should do?"

"About what?" Hollis asked.

"The Experiment in Living. What kind of project should we do?"

Again we were silent. When it seemed obvious that none of us had anything to say on the subject, Stuart continued.

"Actually, I've been thinking about this experiment ever since yesterday. I can't *stop* thinking about it. I hope nobody minds, but to save time, I've written up a plan for us."

"A plan?" Rachel looked up from her book.

"It's rough, of course, and you may have some ideas to add."

"Yes, we just might," she said tartly.

"Good. You see, I'm convinced that the only way to conduct an Experiment in Living is to actually go to the woods and . . . live." Stuart pulled some papers out of his notebook and handed us each a sheet. Across the top in bold block letters was written:

Rachel scanned it quickly and closed *Great Expectations*.

"It's mostly a list," Hollis said. "I thought you said it was a plan."

"The list *is* the plan," Stuart replied. "The list is what we'll take to the woods. It's all Henry David Thoreau took when he moved to Walden Pond, and it's all we're going to take."

"'Rice, molasses, Indian meal, lard, one pumpkin . . .' What on earth are you going to do there?" Rachel asked.

"Live. We're going to do just what Henry David Thoreau did."

I was intrigued by the idea, but Rachel Haygen was not in the least interested. She wanted to be left alone, and the sooner we got this experiment nonsense out of the way, the better.

"Look, Stuart," she said, folding her copy of the contract and tucking it into her book, "there's no need to go to such extremes. I say we research Thoreau's life and write up an in-depth biography. Maybe we can throw in a map of Concord. But actually go to the woods? You're taking this too literally."

"Hey, we could make a three-D map of Walden out of papier-mâché!" Hollis said.

"Don't you mean a topographical map?" Rachel asked distastefully.

He shrugged. "Yeah, I guess so. We could build the

pond and fill it with real water and float little ducks in it. The cabin could be made of twigs and the treetops could be moss."

"And what happens when the water soaks into the papier-mâché and turns it to mush? My, that will be a lovely project. We'll call it Walden Bog."

Stuart was getting impatient. "We don't need to worry about reports or maps yet. Let's just get into the woods as soon as we can. The experiment will work only if we start *thinking* like Henry David Thoreau."

Rachel snorted. "And for this project, for our *grade*, we'll tell Mrs. Stark that we changed our *thoughts*."

"That's right." Stuart handed his pen to Hollis. "Now, if you would all please sign the Henry Contract."

"Oh good grief," Rachel said.

"We really have to sign it?" Hollis asked. "What's this other list for? 'Boards, shingles, hinges, screws'?"

"That's for the cabin we're going to build. If we're going into the woods for six weeks, we'll need some shelter."

"What woods? What cabin?" Rachel cried. "You can't just make decisions for all of us! Who do you think you are?"

Stuart leaned forward, lowered his voice, and looked at each of us steadily. "I'm the one who knows where an ancient forest is, a forest so old Henry David Thoreau's grandfather could have lived there."

"I'll bet," Rachel mumbled, opening *Great Expectations* again.

"Where?" I asked.

"I'll have to take you."

"Well, it had better be close," Rachel said, turning a page. "I can't go too far on school days, even if it is for a school project."

"Does this mean you'll sign? All of you?" Stuart asked. Sixth period was almost over and Mrs. Stark was trying to regain the class's attention.

"I'm in," I said.

"Me too," Hollis echoed. Rachel held out for more details, but in the end she, too, wrote her name across the bottom of the contract.

"We'll meet on Saturday morning at ten o'clock. Can you all get to Middleton Road and Sylvan Shores Drive?" Stuart asked.

"I should be able to," Rachel sniffed. "It's practically across the street from me."

Hollis and I nodded. I passed Sylvan Shores every day on the bus ride home.

"Good, because not far from there is our very own Walden Pond."

Rachel smirked. "Off Middleton Road? I doubt it."

Stuart collected our signed contracts. And seconds later we were swarmed by kids racing out of Mrs. Stark's room to experiment with living.

Chapter 3

"No yard! but unfenced Nature reaching up to your very
sills. A young forest growing up under your windows,
and wild sumacs and blackberry vines breaking
through into your cellar . . . no gate—no front-yard,—
and no path to the civilized world!"

H. D. THOREAU

"This had better be a *real* forest," Rachel warned, stepping
over the ditch and into heavy brush. "I've lived across the
street all my life, and I've never heard of an ancient woods
hidden in here."

When I rode up on my bike Saturday morning and
found Stuart Garfield sitting on the gates of Sylvan Shores
Estates, I'd been disappointed too. Beyond the brick portals
were perfect lawns and row after row of split-level houses, all
neat and trim. Henry would have been appalled.

Stuart pointed to the scrubby patch of woods at the side
of the development. "You'll see, a short hike through those
trees and we'll be at the entrance to Wayburn Woods."

We followed him single file and chest deep through hawthorn bushes, dodging their spikes and red berries, until we were clear of the thicket and came out beneath some alders, our shoes sinking into the leaf mulch and crunching in the layered twigs. Stuart was right. The little stretch of trees off the road was only the neck of the woods. About a half mile in, the narrow strip broadened into a meadow and expanded out to the west until it disappeared. We crossed over the rolling ground and found that the meadow skirted the edge of an enormous three-tiered hill that ended hundreds of feet below at the shore of Wayburn Lake.

We looked down on the cottonwoods along the shoreline. The yellow leaves shimmied and sounded like the applause of a stadium crowd, which was an odd sound to hear in such a remote place. Between the waving branches we could see the silver water of the lake.

Stuart steered us east, and suddenly, like a fortress, Wayburn Woods rose up thick and dark. The trees flowed down to the lake, around its edges, and back seemingly forever. If we had been birds and could have lifted ourselves above the treetops, still we would not have seen the end of Wayburn Woods. It would have stretched out beyond us in green, endless acres.

"Well," Stuart asked, turning to Rachel, "is this real enough for you?"

"It's certainly big enough."

"About ten thousand acres, but that probably isn't too big for the experiment."

"This is private property, you know," Rachel said. "Somebody's going to find out we're here and—"

"He already knows. My dad drove me over to Wayburn Dairy yesterday. Eugene Wayburn himself said it was fine. He even wished us luck."

Rachel was quiet for a few minutes. "Are we going to hike all ten thousand acres, or do you have someplace in mind?" she asked.

Stuart wouldn't say any more. He just smiled and led us through sweet fern and elderberry bushes. We passed into crowds of birches so thick, I could connect them with my outstretched arms. We must have made a huge racket on that first day we came crashing into Wayburn. In a place as still as that, every human sound is magnified—the swish of our blue jeans, the slight wheeze in Rachel's breathing. But the deeper we went, the more Wayburn swallowed everything up. Even Stuart Garfield looked small on the rise up ahead, where he finally stopped and motioned to us.

I suppose every forest has a center, a place where the idea of the forest first began. We had found the center of Wayburn Woods, primeval and mossy, dark and calm, where some glacier a thousand centuries back had dragged its belly and carved out the lake's basin. Wayburn Woods felt wild and sacred at the same time, like a museum and a cathedral all rolled into one. The sunlight came down in pillars, as broad and round as the trees themselves. All around us in the air were particles of leaf and bark, swimming like plankton in a pale green sea.

Hollis spotted an enormous fallen oak, looking like

a moss-covered submarine, lying across the grove. He scrambled up its side. The soft, rotting bark fell away in clumps.

"It's like a giant's land!" he shouted from the top. "There could be all kinds of giant things in here! Giant birds, caterpillars, frogs!" He paused. "Hey, you think maybe we've passed into some other dimension, and that's why these trees seem so big?"

"No," Rachel said flatly. "I think you should come down. The altitude up there is affecting your brain."

For a while Rachel seemed untouched by Wayburn. She sat on a stump next to Hollis's tree and pulled *Great Expectations* from her pocket. But soon she put her book away and was running her hand along the sun-speckled ferns that tucked themselves against the decaying trunk.

We named this part of the woods the Old Grove and began the search for a cabin site. Rachel found it. Stuart, Hollis, and I had been racing around looking for an open space, when she climbed a knoll above us and said, "This is it." No one could argue. From there we could see the open water of Wayburn Lake and the entrance to an inlet below. We couldn't see the actual shoreline, and Hollis was thrilled because that meant no one could see us from the banks of the inlet, either.

"Which is a real advantage in case somebody should arrive by boat. From out in the lake, the trees will shield the cabin from view, and if they pull up onshore, the ridge will protect us. It's a great defensive position."

"Who would want to attack us?" I asked.

"You never know. When the other kids in Stark's class see this, we could have real trouble."

I couldn't imagine that we would be the envy of other students, or that they would launch a fleet of boats to find us.

"It is a great location, but mainly because we'll be able to watch the water, like Henry David Thoreau did," Stuart said. We sat under the birches on the knoll, and he read a chapter to us called "The Ponds" from an unabridged copy of *Walden* he had in his jacket.

> "Walden is a perfect forest mirror, set round with stones as precious to my eye as if fewer or rarer. Nothing so fair, so pure, and at the same time so large, as a lake, perchance, lies on the surface of the earth."

Mrs. Stark would have been pleased to see what a faithful student Stuart was: he read just as sincerely in the middle of the woods as he did in class. I leaned back and watched the burgundy oak leaves against the sky. Henry went on about the water bugs and fish, and the railroad that flanked the pond and how men were improved just by getting a glimpse of Walden Pond from the window of the train. I could have listened to Stuart all day. His enthusiasm wasn't as annoying in the forest somehow. Rachel, however, didn't like being read to, especially four or five pages.

"Look, shouldn't we get started on this cabin? Thanksgiving is a long way off, but I don't like waiting until the last minute on projects that will count for most of my grade."

Our cabin was going to be as simple as Henry's. We would sink four corner posts into the ground and connect them with horizontal braces. Then we'd build walls, running the boards lengthwise as we went. If that didn't feel sturdy enough, we'd pound more braces into the dirt and secure them vertically to the walls. We decided the roof should be pitched so that rain could run off and Stuart could stand up straight.

"How much wood do we have?" Rachel asked.

"Actually, we don't have any," Stuart said. "Not yet."

Hollis placed a stick where the front door was to be and we began using it to enter and exit, as if the walls were already solid. We paced around the floor plan and finally admitted that finding and transporting that much lumber this distance was a daunting if not impossible task.

"Maybe we should just get a tent," Hollis said.

"Absolutely not. Thoreau had a cabin at Walden Pond, and we have to have one too." I would have expected Stuart to say this, but incredibly it was Rachel talking. She heaved herself up resignedly and brushed off the bottom of her jeans. "Come on, then. My dad will give us the wood. He'll give us everything we need." Then she left by the imaginary front door.

Halfway down the slope she stopped. "Well, are you coming or not?"

The Haygen house was a landmark on Middleton Road. You couldn't miss the huge, battered house, which served the community as a handy point for giving directions to strangers. The circular driveway was obscured by overgrown bushes and rusty tricycles. Whenever we drove by it, my mother always said, "Can you imagine what it must have been like in its heyday?" I couldn't imagine, because now in its low day, it was a shambling old man of a house.

Rachel led us through a side door into the kitchen, where two skinny little boys were loading a dishwasher. They looked us over curiously; I don't think Rachel had brought many school friends through that door.

"Where's Dad?" she asked them.

"He's on the 'zebo," replied the one with grape juice stains on his chin. She wound us through a foyer stacked high with apple crates and into a family room where a Ping-Pong table held piles of folded laundry and a television. We found Mr. Haygen on a gazebo that opened onto the back lawn and the shores of Hawthorn Lake. My mother should have seen that! Even I could picture the turn-of-the-century garden parties that must have swirled around it when the Haygen house had been a summer home to some wealthy Detroit family.

Now the gazebo housed enough logs and kindling for ten winters and scrap lumber piled nearly to the rafters. In the middle, up to his ankles in sawdust, Mr. Haygen worked a table leg on a lathe. Rachel had some quiet words with him and he looked up, beaming.

"So you kids are building a fort, eh?" He pulled his glasses off, still smiling and nodding his head in approval.

Stuart offered him his hand. "Mr. Haygen, I'm Stuart

Garfield. This is Beth Gardner, Hollis Robbins. We're working with Rachel on a school project out in Wayburn Woods.
We'd really appreciate it if you could help us out with some
lumber, sir." Stuart's enthusiasm was working wonders on
Rachel's father.

I guess it was the "sir" and Stuart's casual diplomacy
that caused Hollis and me to stand there speechless and
respectful while the grown-ups talked it over. Mr. Haygen
was obviously elated that his daughter was in the company of
such fine young people.

We left the Haygen house in a bizarre caravan. Mr. Haygen drove a small tractor that towed a flatbed piled high with
lumber. Even though it was secured with ropes, Hollis insisted
on straddling the mound like an elephant driver. Attached to
the flatbed was a cart holding a cement mixer into which we'd
piled short lumber, hammers, saws, and nails. Rachel and I
rode on the caboose, holding on to the cement mixer, while
Stuart ran ahead to determine the best route.

Mr. Haygen towed us across the meadow and stopped at
the tree line because Wayburn Woods was too dense for even
a small tractor to pass through. For over an hour we marched
in and back again, toting boards and plywood, until we had
unwittingly beaten down the first path into the Old Grove.

Under Mr. Haygen's supervision, our cabin went up
quickly. By late afternoon the walls were up, the forest closed
out, and the warm, secret feeling of a shelter set in. There
were compromises. Because of a warped board, we moved
the door from the lake side to face the Old Grove. Hollis was

concerned but figured his senses would sharpen after some time in the woods, and that he would be able to hear the invading boats scrape along the beach even if he couldn't see them from the doorway.

He also wanted to pile fallen pine boughs on the roof to give it the shaggy look of the Swiss Family Robinson's tree house.

"Don't be ridiculous. It was a Pacific island. All the Robinsons *had* were palm leaves," Rachel said.

"Right, and pine branches are what we have, so we should use them here," Hollis replied.

"But they were shipwrecked, remember?" Rachel said. "It's not like we're stuck here. We can go to the hardware store or my dad's shop and use anything we want. Whoever heard of covering up perfectly good plywood with branches!"

Hollis wanted to pretend we were shipwrecked. I did too. Wayburn Woods was starting to feel like an island, remote and safe and far from the hallways of Pine Brook School.

The sun was nearly gone when Stuart called us in for a meeting. Mr. Haygen had offered to pull us back on the flatbed, and he waited on the ridge while Stuart assembled us inside.

"I know this isn't quite how Walden was built. Henry David Thoreau had outside help, but not as much as we've had."

"This dirt floor won't do for long," Rachel said. "The

first rain we get, it will soften up like cake frosting. And we need a hinged door to keep the wind out."

"With a lock," Hollis added.

Rachel continued to analyze the interior critically, citing all kinds of deficiencies that would make life in the cabin miserable once the serious winter weather arrived. To me it seemed pointless to make the cabin weather-tight when the Experiment in Living would be over by Thanksgiving. November in central Michigan is not exactly Siberia, but no one else seemed to notice that.

"We couldn't have done this without your dad, Rachel. It was really generous of him to help so much. We'll have to find a way to pay him back."

As always, Hollis and I mumbled our appreciation in the wake of Stuart's eloquence. Rachel smiled shyly, proudly. I could see Mr. Haygen through a gap in the wall. He was leaning against a tree, smoking a pipe and blowing white clouds into the dark air. Anybody could see we'd already paid him back.

Chapter 4

"Not till we are lost, in other words,
not till we have lost the world, do we
begin to find ourselves . . ."
H. D. THOREAU

Hollis peered suspiciously into the bubbling pot. "What is that?"

"Breakfast," Stuart replied, "Henry David Thoreau–style."

"I thought old-fashioned breakfasts had things like eggs and bacon, pancakes and syrup."

Hollis was right to worry about the yellow paste that Stuart was stirring over a small campfire. When he had told us to be at the cabin by eight o'clock on Sunday morning for an historic breakfast, no one had imagined the big surprise would be mush. But that's just what he plopped onto some old tin plates and handed to us.

"I was supposed to use Indian meal, but they didn't have any at the F and P. They'd never even heard of it. I had to use cracked corn instead. Try some molasses on it."

"Cracked corn is what you feed ducks!" Hollis wouldn't even try the cereal and kicked his way around the cabin while the rest of us nibbled at it stoically.

"I thought Henry made cakes out of Indian meal and cooked them on sticks," Rachel said.

"He did. I thought this would be easier, you know, like oatmeal."

"Oatmeal would have been better," Hollis muttered from the side of the cabin.

Stuart emptied the contents of his F&P bag on the ground. The outlook for lunch didn't look much better. He spread out rice, rye meal, bacon, flour, sugar, a can of lard, apples, sweet potatoes, a small pumpkin, salt, and the molasses.

"Don't look so shocked. This is our contract food. There's nothing here that wasn't listed in the Henry Contract," Stuart said.

"Somehow it looks worse out here," I observed.

Rachel hefted the lard can and studied the other groceries for a while. "I'll handle lunch," she finally said.

We sat outside the cabin and read aloud from Stuart's copy of *Walden*. This time we all took turns. The chapter was called "Where I Lived, and What I Lived For" and turned out to be a longer version of what Henry had written in our literature book. For pages and pages Henry walked. There wasn't a field or a farm within twelve miles that he didn't know well. I thought about my own little pathways, the distances I travel every day from home to school, from locker to classroom. What amazed me was how big Henry had made his world; he was out learning the whole countryside.

"It's time we split up," Stuart said, closing *Walden*. "We should spend the rest of the day by ourselves."

"Why?" Hollis asked.

"So we can start the experiment."

Hollis looked confused. "I thought we had started. We've got the cabin, the food."

"That's just the beginning."

"This must be the part where we change our thoughts," Rachel said as she gathered up the plates. "I don't know about my *thoughts*, but I'll do my best to improve the food."

We all felt a little awkward standing around the cabin door, not knowing where to go. Hollis seemed especially bewildered. Stuart, the first to leave, gathered up a big roll of brown butcher paper he'd brought and a bag of supplies.

"See you at lunch," he said, and walked down the slope to the Old Grove. Rachel disappeared into the cabin to sort out the food, and Hollis wandered off into the birches.

I hadn't a clue where to go, but I went down to the lake, pretending that I did. I followed the shoreline as it curved and flattened into a cattail marsh. I'd brought a pen and notepad, thinking I might write about the forest like Henry had. The sun flashed on the lake like pieces of broken mirror. Under the trees, the mottled autumn leaves had gently collided and lay in ruin. I saw plenty to write about, but the impressions were too fragile to copy down in clunky words.

After several hours I came back, cautiously, as an outsider might, and stood above the cabin and the Old Grove. From there I could see Stuart pacing around, counting trees, and jotting something down in his notebook. Rachel was feeding the fire and fussing with a bunch of pots and lids. It occurred to me that maybe my role in the experiment was a reporter. Maybe just watching and recording what everyone else did would be my experiment.

I doubled back to the cattail marsh and retraced my route along the shore. There I found Hollis halfway up the slope, intent on finding dead bugs. He was searching under rocks and sifting the soil with his fingers.

"A whole carcass would be the best find," he told me, "but anything—legs, heads, abdomens, wings—will help me solve the mystery."

"There's a mystery?" I asked.

"I think this slope was an insect highway," he said. "The insects used it to escape the lake animals—fish, turtles, birds, and whatnot. They migrated up this hill to reach the higher ground, to be safe."

"I didn't know insects moved in groups."

"Not groups. I think it was probably individual bugs who made the journey, the courageous ones who were willing to brave the slope and start a new life."

He let me hold the most important discovery of the day,

a grasshopper's skeleton, minus its head, bleached white and still clinging to a leaf fragment. Hollis's theory of bug heroes sounded silly to me, but it was awfully trusting of him to let me hold his best piece of evidence.

From the cabin door Rachel bellowed out that lunch was ready. We sat around the campfire while she served us each an ash-covered sweet potato. With Stuart's pocketknife she split them open and dabbed each one with lard. Hollis was ecstatic.

"Now, this is more like it. No offense, Stuart, but this looks like actual food."

"You haven't seen the main course yet." Rachel lifted the lid of Stuart's cooking pot and showed us the rice she'd cooked with bits of bacon and wild onion. "I think you'll notice the herbs make all the difference. I found the wild onion in the meadow."

"How do you know so much about plants?" Hollis asked.

She took a book from her back pocket and held it up.

"Botanical field guide. I brought it along for something to do and it came in handy. The shepherd's purse was easy to find. Once I recognized it, it turned up everywhere. Sometimes it's called pepper-and-salt. Let's hope for good reason."

We were starved, but Rachel held on to the forks.

"I guess I should probably show you the dessert now, so there won't be any suspense." She removed the lid of the smaller pot with a flourish.

"Apple cobbler. I made a topping by cutting the lard into

the flour. Then I sweetened it with molasses and put it on the sliced apples and baked it until it softened up. Actually, I think it turned out pretty well."

"Pretty well" was an understatement. We ate every crumb. Stuart even suggested that we add the apple cobbler recipe to the terms of the Henry Contract. Hollis and I agreed. Rachel blushed and poked at the fire.

After lunch, Hollis told us that he wanted to dig trenches up the hillside and construct a system of running water for the cabin, as he'd seen in *The Swiss Family Robinson*.

"How could it possibly work?" Rachel asked.

"The Robinsons used wheels and pulleys, and little cups, probably coconut shells, that scooped water up from the lagoon and carried it like a ski lift up to the tree house." Hollis gestured in big, vague motions to show how a similar plumbing arrangement could ascend our slope.

"Coconut shells. Now, that's something we have an abundance of," said Rachel.

"We could use tin cans."

"It'll never work," Rachel decided.

"We don't need running water," Stuart said. "There are a lot of things we don't need. That's the whole point."

We left the woods before dusk, promising Stuart that we would keep our minds in Wayburn Woods even though we were being forced back to civilization. He reminded us that since we had signed the contract, we were honor bound to stay faithful to the experiment until we met again on Monday after school. I wasn't really sure how to do that, but as I rode home in the fading light, I decided to stay away from the television and any other luxuries that might distract me. I figured that if it was something Henry didn't need, then I didn't need it either.

Mother was there when I got home. She was standing in the kitchen wearing a kimono-style bathrobe and some worn-out ballet slippers, but she still looked elegant. She always does. She's especially dazzling at school functions like back-to-school nights and glee club concerts. At those gatherings she really stands out from the stodgy mothers. Most people say I look just like her, but I don't see it. Her dark hair and eyes look as if an artist had traced them with a fine pen.

"Congratulate me," she said, winking. "Your mother sold another house today."

"Does that make you an official agent?"

"Oh no. I have to finish my course work and take a Realtor's exam. Then I'll have my license. But I'm learning to handle offers and counteroffers, and I'm getting bonuses for every sale that I assist." She straightened the collar of my jacket.

While I had been in Wayburn Woods all day, she had been wading through someone's flower bed, hammering in McDuff Realty Open House signs, and serving coffee. I felt an emotion tug at me that I couldn't identify.

"We're going to buy you some new fall clothes, Elizabeth. I don't like you looking so ragtag."

I was low on clothes. When our money ran out, I'd sprung up a few inches and right out of my old things. It was getting harder every morning to put together outfits that fit the standards of most Pine Brook School girls. I didn't care though, especially now. Mother rambled on about matching sweater sets and boots, but I looked out the window and willed myself across Middleton Road, to the Old Grove, to the cabin, to Henry. I was already eager to get back to the woods, back where jeans and an old jacket were perfectly in style.

I began my journal that night. I wrote long after Mother had gone to bed and the furnace had creaked to a halt. I leaned into the warmth of my bedside lamp and wrote about our experiment in Wayburn Woods. Nothing eluded me this time; the events of the day spilled out of my pen in a clear stream of words. Around midnight I turned off the light, but I couldn't sleep, for the stream was still running strong and noisily through me.

Chapter 5

"With respect to luxuries and comforts, the
wisest have ever lived a more simple and
meagre life than the poor."

H. D. THOREAU

On Monday morning I realized that one weekend in Wayburn Woods had already changed me. As I walked down the aisle of the bus, the seats seemed smaller, the ceiling lower. Even the interior of Pine Brook School was different. Had the hallways always been this narrow and stuffy? Another thing puzzled me: I had showered and shampooed away every trace of Wayburn Woods, but all morning I caught whiffs of oak bark and campfire smoke as thin and fleeting as thoughts. When I least expected it, in the middle of homeroom while Mr. Koenig read the daily bulletin, there would be the damp, mossy smell of the Old Grove.

And after lunch, as I climbed the stairs to Mrs. Stark's classroom, things became even stranger. In the hallway a crowd had gathered around Cindy Wedford and Kathy Dulack, which wasn't unusual. But this time the onlookers were shrieking in disbelief. Pine Brook's two finest models of fashion and status were not wearing their Glamma Girl clothes.

Glamma Girl outfits were the uniform of popular girls. The standard issue was capri pants with matching tops. A true Glamma Girl wore these through every season, layering on Glamma sweaters and jackets when the weather cooled. There were Glamma shoes, socks, underwear. The ideal was to have nothing but Glamma fabric touch your entire body. They were expensive clothes, and to make sure everyone knew they were the real thing, every Glamma item was branded with a little *G*. And now Kathy and Cindy had done the unthinkable: they were wearing ordinary clothes like the rest of us. Kathy had disguised herself in a plain sweatshirt and jeans. Cindy had on khaki pants and a turtleneck.

"These cargo pants are my mom's, and this top—are you ready for this? The turtleneck is my *grandmother's*!" Cindy screeched. "She wears it to her bowling club!"

"Are you out of your mind?" someone said.

"Has Larry seen you?"

"I can't believe you came like this!"

"It's for the Experiment in Living," Cindy explained. "We're dressing *simply*." Then she and Kathy flounced into the room wearing their un-Glamma clothes.

34

They had done this for Henry! I looked for Stuart's reaction, but he was dutifully following Mrs. Stark's lesson on adverbs. Rachel was reading *The Time Machine* and was paying just enough attention to avoid being caught. Hollis was four seats behind me and impossible to see, so I couldn't share my disgust with anyone until that afternoon when we met at the cabin.

"They're not experimenting," I told Stuart. "They're doing this to get attention. It has nothing to do with Henry!"

"Probably not, but at least they're trying," he said.

"How can you call it trying? They've twisted it all around. Don't you see what will happen? Pretty soon it will become stylish to wear what is unstylish. They're using the experiment to make themselves even more popular!"

Stuart considered my theory. "It may be the closest they'll ever get to understanding Henry David Thoreau. We should feel sorry for them, Beth. We really should."

But I couldn't feel any sympathy for Cindy Wedford and Kathy Dulack. And sure enough, by Tuesday morning more girls in Cindy's group began wearing common clothes from their mothers' and sisters' closets. Denim skirts with blouses, blazers and slacks—as long as the celebrated *G* wasn't on the garment, then it was "simple" living. The boys joined in and soon the trend mutated into mismatched, crazy combinations, like T-shirts with bow ties.

When Ben Jones showed up on Thursday in his baseball jersey and pajama bottoms, Mrs. Stark stepped in.

"I'm pleased," she began, "that so many of you have

embraced the spirit of Mr. Thoreau's philosophy of simple living. I'm sure he would be"—here she coldly assessed Larry Duncan, who wore a Hawaiian shirt and a striped silk tie—"very impressed with your sincerity. Kathy, Cindy, you may continue your clothing experiment since it was yours originally. But the rest of you had better confine this sort of dressing up to Halloween."

I really couldn't gloat much though, as we were having our own troubles with simplicity in Wayburn Woods. On Tuesday we discovered that Mr. Haygen had used his day off to remodel the cabin. He installed wooden floorboards and a small potbellied stove that had been in his basement. He bored up through the roof to add a smoke pipe, then placed the stove on a platform of bricks. Next to the stove he had even stacked some kindling. Lastly, he filled our misshapen doorway with a carved oak door. I guess Mr. Haygen wanted very much to see his daughter and her upstanding young friends make it through the winter.

We were so astounded by the sudden permanence of our cabin that Stuart amended the Henry Contract and announced that we could bring furniture. With a stick he drew the dimensions of our cabin in the dirt.

"Here's the deal," he said. "We can have only a bed, a table, a desk, and three chairs—no more than Henry David Thoreau had." We decided a fourth chair would be more useful than a bed, and the table could serve as the desk. "But that's all," Stuart said. "And remember, keep it simple."

I donated a broken-down lawn chair. Rachel's little brothers carried a card table and two antique parlor chairs through the woods.

Stuart brought a lantern with a candle inside. "We really do need some light now when the door's closed."

Hollis surprised us all. He pulled a wagon through Wayburn Woods and unloaded three TV trays, a clock, a breadbox, a red leather barstool, and an oil painting of some mallard ducks. "I thought it would make the place kind of homey," he said.

Stuart accepted it all patiently, even though the clearing in front of the cabin was looking like a yard sale. A light rain was falling, so we stayed inside and arranged furniture until the sun began to set. All those chairs were making walking difficult, and we could maneuver only if we took turns. That evening we read *Walden* by the light of the lantern and listened to the rain hitting the leaves. Later we went into the Old Grove to watch the candle glowing through the seams of the cabin walls.

But rain continued all week, and the temptation to bring things to Wayburn Woods became overwhelming. By Thursday a steady flow of toys littered the cabin. We brought a dart board, magazines, modeling clay, puzzles, anything to cover the growing realization that there wasn't much to do in Wayburn Woods when the weather turned bad.

Our new stove was a disappointment. We couldn't find enough dry wood to sustain a fire, and Rachel's repeated attempts made the cabin so smoky that we were driven outside, where we stood around cold and miserable, trying to avoid the dripping branches.

Our intentions to think and act like Henry were all but forgotten. By Friday our greatest chore was the dreary, soggy trek to the cabin, where we punched in like tired employees and put in our time. That afternoon Stuart found Monopoly money mixed into the birch leaves outside the doorway. He walked in with a stricken face, the blue bills clenched in his fist.

"Do you know what this means?" he asked. Hollis and I looked up from a game of Scrabble.

"It means we're killing the whole experiment. We're killing Henry David Thoreau with all this junk!" He upset a TV tray, and a pile of origami papers sifted down like gaudy leaves around his feet.

He turned and left, banging the oak door shut, but it bounced wide open, leaving a gaping hole in the curtain of rain. After he had gone, we saw what had driven him away. The cabin looked like the playroom of some incredibly spoiled and restless child. We tried to tidy up, stacking and repositioning our various diversions in the corners, but it was no use. We simply had too much stuff.

"Hey, he forgot the reading," Hollis said. "He left before we read from *Walden*." But nobody felt like reading; anyway, it was Stuart who chose the chapter and made sure everyone took a turn. And it was Stuart who was always holding up the Henry Contract and making sure we all followed the rules. We blew out the candle and left the woods early, though the heavy clouds made it seem much later. At Middleton Road, Rachel crossed without a wave and Hollis just kept shrugging and burrowing down deeper into his jacket.

I assumed the whole thing was over. I had a spiral notebook full of journal entries describing our experiment, but they were pointless now. On the way home I planned out a new project, a solo project. Maybe I'd make a diorama out of a shoe box, create a little forest with construction paper. Then Mrs. Stark could peek in and see the experiment that never was.

The rain may have shut us down in Wayburn Woods, but it sure hadn't dampened my mother's rising career in real estate. Once again she had been the hostess of an open house and this time had landed the sale of a six-bedroom contemporary on Myrtle Lake.

"Another bonus will be on the way, but even more important, it seems I'm attracting the attention of the main office," she said.

"And that's a good thing?" I asked.

"It's a wonderful thing. The Detroit office oversees our branch and decides our *salaries*," she answered, smiling.

At the kitchen table she told me about the splendid high-rise headquarters of McDuff Realty, where Mr. McDuff himself made appearances. I wasn't sure why that was such a big deal, but she was excited, and it had been a long time since she had been excited about anything.

I found Henry in the encyclopedia on Saturday morning. I copied his birth date, the day he graduated from Harvard College, and the day he began working in his father's pencil factory. I even cut a peephole in a shoe box, but that's as far as it went. I just couldn't cut out little paper trees when the giant oaks of Wayburn, as massive as locomotives, were steaming in the sunlight, their branches dark and shining.

I went back to Wayburn Woods not expecting to see anyone, but before I reached the trailhead above the Old Grove, I heard voices. Rachel's two youngest brothers were busily strapping rope and canvas around what looked like a small Conestoga wagon. They were about to haul all the Haygen junk back to its source. Rachel was directing the operation from the cabin door with a spatula.

"What's taken you so long?" she shouted at me. "I've held up breakfast for nearly an hour." Stuart waved from below in the Old Grove. He was bent over the stump of the submarine tree, intent on his brown paper scroll. The experiment was still alive; I needed a few minutes to take it all in.

Later I learned that Rachel had been responsible for scrubbing the cabin clean of our modern clutter. Only the furniture survived. By the time I arrived, she had stoked a hot fire and was flipping pancakes in a cast-iron skillet. I did notice one new addition. On the wall she had hung a few castoff pots and cooking utensils from the Haygen house, and beside the stove she'd set up a wooden crate as a pantry.

"Look, even Thoreau had cooking supplies. I needed some equipment if we were going to keep eating out here.

It's bad enough I have only these weird ingredients to work with."

We ate outside in the sun that poured over Wayburn Woods. The combination of a hot breakfast and clear weather made Hollis so happy he couldn't sit down.

"You know, we're finally getting the hang of this," Hollis said through a mouthful of pancakes. "Living like HDT and all."

"So it's HDT now?" Rachel said, flipping three more pancakes onto his plate.

Hollis nodded. "Sure, why not?" In between bites he told us about the insect display he was organizing for his Henry project.

"I've labeled their parts, and I'm going to show that the forest floor is like a graveyard. Insect bodies are all over the place." Before the junk wagon had departed for the Haygen house, he had salvaged a cigar box and made it into a show-case for his relics. His finest specimens—the bleached grass-hopper, the filigree of dragonfly wing, the leg of a walking stick, the moth head—he placed in a velvet box that had once held a wristwatch. It clicked shut on metal hinges like a tiny coffin.

Rachel's role in our Experiment in Living was also secured. Maybe her whole life had been preparing her for this moment when she would convert Henry's meager diet into edible food for us. We compared her gift for cooking to her father's skill in carpentry; the Haygen Approach, we called it.

After breakfast Rachel walked down the reedy bank

below our compound to where the inlet became swampy. She pulled up an armful of the cattails that grew thickly there, and then sat at the water's edge, stripping off their outer stems. She consulted her field guide, then sliced off the tops until she had a pile of the long, tapered roots.

"If you're in a hurry," she told me, "you can eat these like celery, or you can pickle them in vinegar or boil them like a vegetable, which is what I'm going to do." We ate cattail heart soup and cattails with rice and mashed cattails that day without complaint. And when she had exhausted the cattails, she began on the acorns.

"The acorns," Rachel said, "will be our salvation. They'll see us through the winter. As long as we have acorns, we'll never starve." I suppose the sheer number of acorns inspired Rachel. In the Old Grove the white oaks had shed bushels of them. We walked on carpets of acorns.

"Just make sure you leave some for the squirrels," Stuart advised.

Of course, Rachel knew all about the dangers of over-foraging. She gathered acorns in a bucket throughout the Old Grove and from a younger grove of oaks to the west. Before Thanksgiving she was going to roast them, grind them, bake them into cakes, boil them into gruel, and brew them into coffee.

I added two to three pages a day to my journal. Already I had over thirty pages on our Experiment in Living, far more than Mrs. Stark's class would ever want to hear. It seemed I often had more leisure time than anyone else in the woods.

Maybe it was because I was sitting alone and idle on the ridge that Stuart singled me out to see his secret project late that afternoon.

"Can I show you my map, Beth?" he asked, unrolling it on the ground. He had mapped out all of Wayburn Woods, from its beginnings on Middleton Road, to the three-tiered hill, to the vast woods beyond. He had drawn it as if he had hung suspended from the clouds, high enough to show the awesome size of Wayburn and low enough to show every tree and stump in the Old Grove. It was astonishingly bold and accurate, as though an architect or an engineer or a genius had drawn it.

"What do you think?" he asked.

"It's incredible," I said, though the word was wholly inadequate. His map was a masterpiece.

He leaned over it, pointing up to the far corner. "See? This legend shows the exact distances between the big oaks in the grove. Well, almost exact, give or take a few inches." He turned to me and smiled. We were sitting so close on the ground that the sleeves of our jackets brushed as he reached across the paper.

"And these symbols represent important places. Here's where Rachel harvested the cattails today, and here's the hill where Hollis found the insect battlefield. Here's the submarine tree and the shortcut path behind the cabin." For some reason I was finding the shape of his face more interesting than the symbols, as if the map showed more about Stuart than it did the forest. It struck me then that it wasn't the map that was incredible; Stuart was incredible with his kind eyes and expert drawing skills. He must have felt me watching him, because he stopped talking. His serious expression softened.

"Do you think the class will like it?" he asked. I didn't care if the class liked it or not. I didn't want the class to even see it. This was our map, our world. Why did we have to parade our Henry projects in front of Mrs. Stark and the class, anyway?

"I honestly don't think you need to show it to the class, Stuart. Maybe you could just hang it in the cabin."

"What? This is my project. This is our Experiment in Living. Why would I hide it out here now that it's finished?"

"Finished! The experiment isn't over for at least a month," I said.

"I know that. I just meant we shouldn't try to hide what we've done out here. We've come closer to thinking and living like Henry David Thoreau than anyone else. I'm sure of it."

I wasn't. Henry had gone to the woods for two years and lived alone; we'd been out here barely two weeks and had split it up four ways. Henry was beyond caring what his neighbors thought, and I was starting to care a great deal what Stuart Garfield thought. More and more Stuart and Henry were getting jumbled up in my mind, and I couldn't tell where one stopped and the other began. All I knew for certain was that the experiment was becoming too personal to share with my sixth-period English class.

"That may be," I said. "But we can't sum up an Experiment in Living in five minutes of show-and-tell. We can't treat Henry like a book report."

Stuart didn't think presenting his project was ridiculous, though. He was proud of that map and called Rachel and Hollis over to see it too. Rachel huffed up from the lake with a bucket of acorns she'd cracked and rinsed.

"We're having too many meetings, Stuart," she said, wiping her wet hands on her jeans. "I've still got another bushel of acorns to hull." She halted when she saw the map spread out and pushed her glasses up.

"Wow!" Hollis squatted down to get a closer look. "This is awesome!"

"Very nice," Rachel said a little stiffly.

"Look, here's the submarine tree!" Hollis exclaimed. "You drew a little periscope on the top; and there's a dragonfly dive-bombing Bug Battlefield!"

"So now that you're finished, what will you do for the next month?" Rachel asked. Stuart lifted his eyebrows to indicate he didn't really know.

"I was wondering how the rest of the projects were coming along," he said. "Maybe now would be a good time for *everyone* to give a progress report."

"I don't recall 'progress reports' being in the contract," Rachel said sharply. "I'm not going to rush my acorn research just because you're done. I can't demonstrate acorn recipes until they've been thoroughly tested."

Hollis looked alarmed. "I'm not near ready, either," he said. "I need lots more carcasses."

I sat silently on my log and refused to take part in the "progress reports." Stuart had his map rolled up tightly and was tapping it against his palm as he stood before us.

"It's just that time goes by quickly and assignments are due before you know it," he said, trying to sound cheerful, but the damage was done. "I didn't mean to make anybody feel rushed."

Actually he hadn't. Rachel hoisted her bucket and went placidly back to the lake. Hollis wasn't overly concerned about getting *any* assignment in on time, let alone this one. But *due dates* and *progress reports* were sour notes to hear in Wayburn Woods. I worried mostly that Stuart was rushing himself. I didn't like the way he paced restlessly around the Old Grove after we left him. Or the way he sighed and frequently glanced up the trail leading home. Just what would he find to do in the woods for all that time? I had the uneasy feeling that he wouldn't find anything.

Chapter 6

"We should come home from far, from adventures,
and perils, and discoveries every day, with
new experience and character."
H. D. Thoreau

Mrs. Stark stood beside her new bulletin board entitled "We Went to the Woods." "As you can see, class, we'll be sharing our Experiments in Living over the course of a week," she said brightly. "Listed here are the groups that will present each day and the order in which they will present." I felt a slow panic rising, a queasiness in my stomach that promised to ruin the month of November. We were scheduled to be the last presenters on Friday. I wasn't sure if that distinction was something to celebrate or not.

"And please note that I've included a running count of the days remaining before Presentation Week. Just a little reminder for those who may be putting off until tomorrow what they could be doing today!" She tore the first numbered page off and declared, "Only twenty-nine days left!"

The dust from that bombshell hadn't settled yet when Mrs. Stark said, "Now, let's open our textbooks to page one-sixty-three and meet another American author, Mr. Nathaniel Hawthorne."

Without a backward glance, we buried Henry under a dozen pages or so. Although we were still experimenting with living, it seemed Mrs. Stark was no longer experimenting with teaching. She wrote our silent reading assignment on the board and then retreated to her desk for the rest of the class period. A long fifty minutes later, just before the dismissal bell, she rose to post our homework pages, but a raised hand stopped her.

"Mrs. Stark," Kathy Dulack said, "I'd like to say something about my Experiment in Living, if that's all right."

"You'd rather not wait until your scheduled time?" Mrs. Stark asked.

"No, this needs to be said now. It's kind of urgent."

"Then go right ahead," Mrs. Stark replied. Kathy's request had caught everyone's attention, but when she stood up and said, "May I go to the front of the room, Mrs. Stark?" we were riveted. Why would anyone volunteer to give a progress report in front of the class?

"You must think I'm awfully foolish," Kathy began sweetly, demurely. "Two weeks ago, when we started this experiment, I really thought that it had to do with clothes and things like that. I was so wrong. You see, something happened to me. It has to do with my great-grandmother. She's in a rest home, Whispering Pines Village. She's ninety-two and really can't do anything for herself anymore. I went to see her last week and she didn't recognize me. She kept calling me Suzanne—that's my mother's name."

I couldn't see what this had to do with Henry, but I was just as mesmerized as the rest of the class by Kathy's voice. The room was in a breathless hush.

"She talked about making roast beef for dinner and about my uncle Richard being on the varsity football team. You see, she thought we were back in the time when my mother was in high school in Louisville."

We waited with her in utter silence, sitting on the edge of the bed while her great-grandmother sorted out the lost decades.

"I realized that Henry Thoreau was right. What we are on the outside doesn't matter. My great-grandmother didn't even recognize me! So that's why, as you can see, I'm not wearing simple clothes anymore. For my experiment I'm going to remember every day that looks just aren't that important."

I agreed completely with Kathy's final point, but the ironic thing was that as she denounced the importance of outward appearances, she had never looked prettier, especially in that peach-colored Glamma Girl sweater and skirt. Every boy must have been filing her image away under the title "Perfection." The bell rang, and as I rose to leave, I saw that none of them regarded her with more admiration than Stuart Garfield.

The rain returned that afternoon. It was coming down so fast, I couldn't see out the bus windows. Rachel sat beside me and read *Kidnapped*. I was grateful actually; the heavy downpour made a bike ride to Wayburn Woods impossible.

"What did you think of that?" I asked Rachel.

She tore her eyes reluctantly from the book. "Think of what?" she said distractedly.

"Kathy's speech."

She shrugged and found her place on the page again. "Coming attractions for the big presentation, I guess."

"And how about that chart of Mrs. Stark's?" I said. "'We Went to the Woods.' That's pretty funny, because I doubt Kathy Dulack has set one toe in the woods."

Rachel was absorbed in *Kidnapped* again, and she didn't answer or look up until we reached her stop. I was left alone with my tangled feelings, a vicious knot of hurt and envy that was pulled hopelessly tighter every time I remembered the way Stuart had stood there by his desk after her speech, his arms by his sides, so enthralled he hadn't even thought to gather up his books until long after the bell had rung.

The bus stopped for me and I ran blindly up our driveway through the rain, which is why I didn't see the strange car parked by the house. What I did see when I got inside was disturbing enough. A man's raincoat was hanging on a peg in the entry hall next to my mother's. From the kitchen came the sound of clinking ice cubes and rich, low laughter. I approached the kitchen cautiously.

"And here she is now!" A broad gray shape moved out of the doorway to let me enter. I had never seen a man in our kitchen before. Sometimes I had tried to imagine my dad leaning against the counter, his feet crossed at the ankle, graceful and handsome. This man in his pin-striped suit and crimson tie appeared as vivid as a cartoon character against the drab cabinets. Mother looked at me proudly, hopefully, wanting me to look more presentable than I did.

"Elizabeth, this is Louis McDuff." *The real estate king!* I smoothed back my drenched hair and smiled limply into his small, friendly eyes.

"How do you do, sir." I sounded like Stuart.

"So this is the young lady I've heard so much about. Your mother and I probably talk more about you than anything else." That hit me as odd. When did they do all this talking? And why wasn't it about selling houses?

"She tells me you're quite a good student."

"Yes, I guess so."

"Nothing more important than getting a good education. The army gave me mine. I was a pilot in Vietnam, troop transports mainly, flew hundreds of runs over some mighty rough terrain. Became somewhat of a hero, you might say, and earned a few medals." Mother was listening with a glowing face, and I had the feeling Mr. McDuff was adding an installment to his ongoing memoirs.

"But the thing I'm most proud of is the college education the army gave me afterward." He crossed his arms and laid them against his generous chest. "No better investment in the world than a college diploma." He fell silent, shaking his head. My mother had the same reverence for college educations, and she sighed wistfully.

I stood cold and wet, listening to the clock tick in the living room and wondering how to excuse myself. It seemed to me that Mr. McDuff had stayed long enough.

He rubbed his hands together. "Isabel, I'm famished. Why don't you ladies get ready to go?"

"Mr. McDuff is taking us out to dinner, Elizabeth."

"A celebration dinner," Mr. McDuff added. "Your mother has single-handedly conquered the market for the East County. One more sale and I'm going to offer her a partnership." He turned to my mother. "If I lost you to the competition, I'd be ruined." Mother and "Louis" laughed as though this were some old joke between them.

I was rushed into my best dress and then ushered into the leather seats of Mr. McDuff's Mercedes-Benz, and off we went to the Hound and Hunter. We pulled under the awning of the plush dining house and valets whisked us into the lobby, where Mr. McDuff's presence sent a maître d' striding to seat us. The thick carpets and brocade seats absorbed all sounds but the tinkling of silver on china.

In this dim, velvety realm, Mr. McDuff was completely at home. We were served course after course, and all the while he gave steady, quiet orders to the scurrying waiters.

The occasion was supposedly to honor Mother's soaring sales record, but Mr. McDuff never mentioned interest rates or escrows. Louis McDuff was interested solely in my mother.

I kept myself entertained with the elegance of the Hound and Hunter. What would Henry say about the butter, molded into the shapes of seashells? What would he say about the silver chalice and the snowball of crushed ice on which my shrimp cocktail was perched? Ha! I knew what he'd say all right. I was smack in the middle of the enemy's camp.

After dinner we strolled into the gift shop and browsed through china figurines, imported chocolates, and those over-size picture books people put on their coffee tables. That's where the Hound and Hunter caught me off guard. There in a pile of books about Renaissance architecture, the Canadian Rockies, and treasures of the Greek isles, I saw a title, *The World of Walden*. On the cover a smooth teal-green lake reflected the trees on its banks. The landscapes were by Thomas Cole and Frederick Church, Hudson River artists. Beside each painting were passages from *Walden* so familiar, it was as though they had been written on the back of my hand.

Mr. McDuff hovered over me, smelling of cologne and brandy and seeming even larger now after his prime rib dinner. He reached down and closed *The World of Walden* in my hands.

"Ah, Thoreau, is it? Do you know who he is?" Mr. McDuff asked. He must have thought the pictures had attracted me.

"I know a little. We're studying him in school."

"A rugged individualist. He marched to the beat of a different drummer, as they say. Someone once said that no truer American existed. Well, I think he's someone you should know more about." Mr. McDuff handed the book to the saleslady and bought it like an after-dinner mint, in spite of my mother's objections.

I sat in the blackness of the backseat while Mr. McDuff drove us home. I wasn't bothered when he whispered words to my mother, which were probably plans for another evening out. I was eager to take the book upstairs and explore it, to show it to Rachel and Hollis and most of all to Stuart. What a prize! It wasn't a book; it was an art museum swimming around Henry's life in the woods, our life in the woods. *The World of Walden*, if possible, was even more beautiful than Kathy Dulack.

The next day I didn't find Stuart in his usual hangout, the drinking fountain by the library stairs, so I waited until after English class to approach him with what I thought would be an irresistible offer. My coffee-table *Walden* was too big to carry to school, so I tried to describe it in words.

"The pictures are paintings, famous ones, not little drawings like in the textbook. And it has all of *Walden* in there too! It's huge!" I was doing a terrible job, but Stuart was always a considerate listener. His eyes widened appreciatively while I stumbled through my sales pitch. Then his attention was drawn to Kathy Dulack, who had quietly joined us and was waiting for me to finish. There was no need to continue. She was so creamy, blond, and captivating that she nearly took my breath away too.

"I'd really like to see that book sometime, Beth. Maybe you could bring it to the cabin," Stuart said. Kathy smiled at me, not unkindly, just distantly.

"This week has gotten kind of busy," Stuart continued, "but I'm going to try to make it out to Wayburn at least once or twice. So maybe I'll see it then."

I had imagined us looking at the paintings together, reading the passages and watching the sky. My face burned with embarrassment. Chip Harris threw his shoulder against Stuart's as he passed by in the hallway. Larry Duncan and Ben Jones punched him in the arm. How had the universe shifted so quickly? In less than twenty-four hours Stuart had not only fallen for Kathy Dulack, but he'd also fallen under the net of her vast social circle.

He smiled uncomfortably and shuffled his long limbs the way he did outside the cabin when he had a difficult announcement to make. But Stuart had started a new experiment. And Kathy, the chief object of that experiment, was expecting to be escorted to class. Her friends were moving off, cuffing one another, calling out to Stuart.

"Three o'clock! By the tennis courts! Don't be late, Garfield!"

I understood why Stuart backed away. He had been chosen. The powerful and popular had reached out to him, and maybe even Henry himself could not have resisted.

Chapter 7

"Our village life would stagnate if it were not for the
unexplored forests and meadows which surround it.
We need the tonic of wildness . . ."
H. D. Thoreau

I think Stuart got bored by popularity. He must have been
bombarded with all kinds of invitations, from bonfires on the
beach to movie dates to video game marathons. I could see
for myself that he was always with Kathy Dulack during
passing periods and pep assemblies and that he ate with all the
important people in the cafeteria. But before long he was
hungry for a new project.

So I wasn't surprised when he became the new editor
of the school paper, the *Pine Press*. I wasn't even surprised when
a few days later he had convinced the principal to give him the
janitor's supply room next to the library for an office. I could
just hear him saying to Mr. Putterman, "Sir, the *Pine Press* needs

to expand so that it can better meet the needs of its students. The newspaper staff needs an office, Mr. Putterman."

And I could just see our principal smiling at this straightforward young man and agreeing to anything he asked. I was only surprised that he didn't give Stuart a secretary from his own office staff. But Kathy Dulack soon took that job, sitting by the door of the newsroom with a sign on her desk that said Editor's Assistant.

Stuart became a visionary in the newspaper business. In no time, he rebuilt that one-page flier into a bulging six-page newspaper. He called an after-school meeting with the English teachers and convinced them to assign feature articles each week. Then he pulled a few strings with his friends on the student council and got money put aside for "feature prizes," rewards for students whose articles were selected for publication. His writing staff was the entire student body! While the rest of us obediently turned out assignments for our English teachers each week, Stuart had permission to sit in his office and cull through piles of our work, choosing articles the *Press* would print.

When a new issue hit the stands, kids went crazy. Having your article selected was like winning the lottery. You not only received passes to football games, coupons for the student store, or free dinners at Blitz's, you also achieved the title of Feature Journalist and your name was added to the list outside the *Press* office. Clearly, Stuart was destined for greater things: he was ready for politics.

Having freed himself from reporting the news, he had

time to develop his favorite section of the *Press*, the editorial page. There Stuart followed tradition and talked about the problems that occupy most school newspapers. He griped about the inferior food in the cafeteria. He argued that the student dress code squelched our creativity. No one could have attacked the no-gum-chewing rule with more energy and imagination. Beyond that, though, he was running out of ideas. And strangely, that's where Henry came back into his life.

Stuart's brief visits to the cabin became scarcer as November began, and we were increasingly startled to see him striding up the trail into the clearing.

"Hey, Stuart!" Hollis said, lifting his head from the cigar box in his lap.

"How are the bug wars?" Stuart asked.

"Not bad. I've invented a new insect. It combines the best features of the hero bugs into the ultimate warrior. I call him Frankensect." Hollis held up the gluey, grotesque shape for Stuart to see.

"Very . . . ingenious," Stuart said diplomatically.

"Nice of you to drop by," Rachel mumbled. She was crushing roasted acorns between two flat rocks.

"Hi, Rachel, Beth." He nodded at us. He was holding his copy of *Walden*. I wondered if he ever thought about our oral reading—if he even remembered which chapter we had read last. He looked out at the lake for a while, but I could see he was troubled.

"Did you know that Henry David Thoreau wrote other things besides *Walden*?" he asked.

"He kept journals," I said, looking up from mine.

"Yes, and he wrote essays too," Stuart replied excitedly. "There's one in my book, at the back, right after *Walden*. It's called 'Civil Disobedience.' You have to hear this!" He opened his book and read:

> "I heartily accept the motto,—'That government is best which governs least'; and I should like to see it acted up to more rapidly and systematically. Carried out, it finally amounts to this, which also I believe,— 'That government is best which governs not at all'; and when men are prepared for it, that will be the kind of government which they will have."

Stuart closed the book. "Isn't that fantastic?"

Hollis's glue bottle made a rude sputtering sound. He shook it vigorously and said, "Personally, I like it better when HDT sticks to the woods; you know, rabbits and birds. No offense, but that government part is sort of boring."

I agreed. The word *government*, the whole idea of government, was as remote as the moon to our lives. As Stuart read, Rachel had begun grinding acorns with such force, I thought sparks might fly. She scraped the mash into a pan and poured in lake water.

"Since it's so great, why don't you use it in your presentation?" she said. "Why don't you add it to your *map*?" I heard the sarcasm in her voice, but Stuart was too preoccupied to notice.

"No, not my map. Building the cabin and being out here

in the woods is fine, but what I'm realizing is that 'Civil Disobedience' is . . . bigger and more important than Henry David Thoreau's experiment at Walden Pond. Looking back, we really should have done our experiment on that instead of spending so much time out here."

"How can you say that?" I burst out.

"Because 'Civil Disobedience' is the most valuable thing Henry David Thoreau ever wrote. You should read it," Stuart urged. "He tells how one individual can change the world just by doing the right thing. *Everyone* should know about this!"

Rachel started for the cabin. She was boiling acorns into acorn coffee and had wasted enough time. "Publish it in your newspaper," she called loudly from inside. "Then everybody's sure to know about it."

Stuart took her advice, using the next editorial in the *Pine Press*:

That School Is Best Which Controls Students Least

Can there be a school where right and wrong are not determined by the administrators, but by the conscience of the students? Must we always let our principal and vice principal make moral decisions for us? Why bother to have a conscience if you're not going to use it? I say we should be people first and students second. Our administrators and teachers want us to respect the *rules,* but I believe it's more important to respect what is *right*! The *Press* hereby recommends that every student throw away his student handbook. Be guided by your conscience, not a rule book!

"I don't know how he gets away with this," Rachel said. She tossed the new edition of the *Press* onto our pile of kindling. "He's promoting anarchy. And he should have written, 'his or *her* student handbook.'"

Anarchy didn't follow his editorial, though. The piece that should have started a revolution turned out to be a dud. Pine Brook readers preferred it when Stuart railed against those stupid rules. They enjoyed his clever arguments for why students *should* dye their hair unnatural colors. Was he now saying they should be so good that rules weren't necessary? That didn't sound like much fun. He had also used the word *conscience* three times in one paragraph, and quite honestly, that was a little unsettling to most. His main idea, his lofty challenge to be better people, had soared right over them.

Stuart soon made another appearance at the cabin. Supposedly he had come to check a few details on his map, but he sat on the fallen log and didn't even slide the rubber band off it. Obviously he'd come for more advice.

"I know I'm on the right track," he told us. "If I could just find an issue that students care deeply about, then we could try out some civil disobedience. What I need is an injustice, something at school that's outrageously unfair."

"There's your problem, right there," Rachel said, pouring dark liquid from a pot. "Kids mainly care about dress code restrictions—no spaghetti straps, no baseball caps, no flip-flops—"

"And no skateboards," Hollis added. "Nobody likes that."

"Those aren't injustices," I said. "They're inconveniences. In Henry's time human beings were used as *slaves;* they were *owned* by other people. That was why he got angry and wouldn't pay his taxes. Our literature book also said that he helped runaway slaves escape to Canada even though it was illegal. To have civil disobedience, you have to have a serious problem."

Stuart stared at me for the longest time. "I'm not so sure of that," he said. "Maybe all those little inconveniences add up to a serious problem."

Rachel took a sip of her latest brew of acorn coffee and grimaced. Achieving the right balance of water to acorn meal was tricky, but she was getting closer. "Oh, please. You're not going to compare being a student to being a *slave!*"

That was exactly what he did, and a week later his editorial in the next *Pine Press* blazed across the page:

ENSLAVED!

Fellow students, we've been duped! The petty rules that we so often complain about on these pages have distracted us from the real problem here at Pine Brook

School! While we've been raging about trifles in the student handbook, we've missed the real assault on our personal freedom. Do you know what that is? It's the *building* itself! They should rename this school Pine Brook Prison. Why? Because we're trapped here like rats in a maze. They let us out of one cage when the bell rings and we scurry to our next cage. No wonder kids are tense and overworked. We have no place to relax from the stress of classrooms and homework!

Stuart proposed converting the outdoor courtyard into a student center with couches and lounge chairs, a television, a jukebox, and a snack bar: ". . . a snack bar with all the amenities of your average concession stand," he wrote. "Our stomachs shouldn't be ruled by the bell schedule. Wouldn't it be great to grab a hot dog on the way to algebra or anytime you wanted?"

They were preposterous ideas and everyone loved them. Students hadn't realized how oppressed they were until he spelled it out for them. The editorial page was a hit and stirred up just the sort of discontent Stuart was hoping for. I doubt students were riled up enough to risk their reputations and freedom the way Henry did, but it was a start.

Luckily, Hollis, Rachel, and I didn't feel the least bit oppressed. The time we spent in the woods became the high point of every day. Even Mrs. Stark with her forbidding daily countdown ("Only 20 days left!") couldn't ruin it for us, at least not yet. We began reading *Walden* again, but in a manner that flew in the face of Stuart's old methods. *The World of Walden* was too heavy to pass around, so we laid it open on the card table and rotated around it. The reader had to hunch over it like a monk reading ancient scripture. The two listeners sat in the antique parlor chairs.

"Whoever's reading can go for as long as they want—more than one page even," Hollis insisted. Rachel and I rolled our eyes because Hollis was ready to quit reading the second he spotted a word he didn't know. And it seemed he always got the hard paragraphs, like the one where Henry talks about constellations. When Hollis came to "Cassiopeia's Chair," he made one feeble try and then pushed the book away in frustration.

"Keep going!" Rachel ordered. "Say it as best you can, but keep going. If you stop at every unfamiliar word, you'll never read *anything*!"

We all struggled with the Latin phrases and the references to Greeks. Like Hollis, we found that with practice we could leap over them and not break stride, the way we were learning to leap over brambles and prickly bushes in the woods. We traveled with Henry through fields and streams. He took us to neighboring farms, and we waited while he talked with farmers and considered purchasing land.

"That kills me," Hollis said, "the way he pretends he's shopping for land and then enjoys it for a while and then just walks away." It was an idea worth trying, I thought, to enjoy beautiful places and things without wanting to have them for your own. How would McDuff Realty like it if *that* idea got around!

Sometimes it seemed that Henry forgot about us and took far too long describing the train as it went by on its way to Boston. Often he told us more than we ever wanted to know about Greek philosophers. But he'd finally remember us again and liven things up by pointing out the whippoorwills and screech owls.

When Rachel was reading she'd make us repeat Henry's words, mimicking Mrs. Stark's fondness for choral reading. "Now, class, please repeat for me the strains of the melodious and melancholy hooting owl. 'Hoo hoo hoo, hoorer hoo.'" Hollis and I would obediently stand by our "desks" and shake the cabin with our hoots.

I didn't see Hollis or Rachel much at school. They stayed in the shadows and moved in obscurity throughout the halls and classrooms like shy birds. But when I did find them in the tramping crush of passing periods, we would walk together and quietly chat about the cabin or the steady, frightful approach of Presentation Week.

"Hey, did you catch that?" Hollis asked us after Mrs. Stark's class. "Only fifteen days left."

"Who could miss it?" Rachel snapped. "I detest that calendar! And the way she bellows out the deadline every day! Doesn't she know its antithetical to Thoreau and everything we're trying to accomplish?"

"That's true," I said. "An Experiment in Living shouldn't have this kind of pressure."

We had reached the bottom of the stairs, where we went our separate ways for seventh period.

"'Time is but the stream I go a-fishing in,'" Hollis said, sauntering off toward the science rooms.

Rachel stared after him. "What did you say?"

He paused and said over his shoulder, "It's what HDT says—you know, we read it yesterday. 'Time is but the stream I go a-fishing in.'" He shrugged and looked a little bashful about quoting Henry. Rachel smiled back at me with amazement, and if I wasn't mistaken—pride.

With Stuart it was entirely different. Now that he was a celebrity, I saw him everywhere. Between classes Kathy Dulack towed him around while she talked with her friends, and Larry Duncan and Ben Jones pummeled him incessantly. They kept him in headlocks right up to the doors of their classrooms, releasing him with only seconds to dash to his own room. I had never seen him so loose and slaphappy, especially when you considered the oppressive school environment he was trapped in. No wonder he couldn't see any real injustices at school—he was having too good a time. Injustices are subtle and show up when you least expect them, like the one I saw on Friday.

When I found Rachel in the locker room before our eighth period P.E. class, she was standing by an open locker and staring straight ahead. She appeared to be paralyzed. I rounded the row of lockers and discovered why. Flanking her like hyenas were Cindy Wedford and Gloria Delano. Rachel's only hope of escape was blocked by a third girl named Nancy Storgenson, whose straight yellow hair hung down to her waist.

"So, have you cooked up any new gourmet plant recipes, Rachel?" Cindy asked sweetly.

"No," Rachel mumbled.

"I wish I could taste your acorn soup. It sounds so delicious. What do you call it? Nutty stew?" Cindy flashed amused eyes at her friends, and they laughed.

"Maybe you could try a casserole next time, with sticks or maybe pinecones," Cindy suggested.

Rachel stared into her locker as if some private cavernous hell were opening up before her. I couldn't understand why she didn't respond; the insults were straight off a grade-school playground, but Rachel the voracious reader, Rachel of the indomitable Haygen Approach, was powerless.

"The next time my dad mows the lawn I'll save the cuttings for you, and you can make a nice salad for your friends." Rachel's shoulders trembled, but she made no sound.

Cindy moved closer and with an intimate, confidential voice asked, "Tell us, are acorns your secret for staying so slender?"

I couldn't see Rachel's eyes, but I knew that as she squinted into the black abyss, tears were rolling down her cheeks. Her chin went down. She clutched her white P.E. shirt and shorts to her chest.

I've never gone looking for injustices, but all my life I've been on the lookout for a real live dragon. I thought about that now, watching Cindy's cruelty from behind the wall of lockers. Here at last was the dragon I'd always wanted to face, slithering around in its own sarcastic stench. But I had no idea how to begin slaying such a creature. Swords and shields wouldn't work. To defeat a real dragon, a dragon in Glamma Girl cropped pants and a matching jacket, you have to go in empty-handed.

"Tell us, then," Cindy crooned, "is it your whole-grain acorn diet or climbing up into that tree house with your wilderness friends that keeps you so trim?"

Rachel buried her face in her clothes and leaned toward the empty locker. I'd heard enough. Sword or not, it was time to join in.

"It's not a tree house," I said, rounding the corner briskly. I set my backpack on the bench next to Nancy. "You were referring to our cabin, I assume. The one in Wayburn Woods?" The dragon was surprised and briefly faltered.

"You didn't read *Walden* very carefully, Cindy," I said, adding a touch of Mrs. Stark to my voice. I figured no one ever spoke to the great Cindy Wedford like that. It worked; she flushed and looked away.

While the three girls exchanged disgusted looks and regrouped, I took off my sweater, folded it with elaborate casualness, and kept talking. "No, the cabin is not a tree house. It sits firmly on the ground, surrounded by birch trees. Actually, I'll be describing it in detail for our presentation."

"Well, I'll just be dying to hear about it." Cindy's words felt toxic, definitely dragon breath.

"You should come out and see it for yourself," I said. "The view of the lake is worth the hike. The cabin overlooks an enormous grove of trees. Rachel found the spot for us. Remember that, Rache?" Her head was now completely in the locker; only a nod indicated she had heard.

I went on cheerily. "A tree house would have been impractical, and we were trying to stick to Henry's plan as much as we could. You do remember Thoreau?" I dressed for P.E. in the most unconcerned manner I could muster. Cindy and her entourage had retreated from their triangular attack formation and were slowly backing out. They didn't know what to make of me; neither did Rachel, who withdrew her head from the locker to throw a frightened sidelong look at me.

"What makes you think we'd be interested in your little fort?" Cindy sneered. She narrowed her eyes and looked at me hatefully.

That's when I discovered that she wasn't a dragon after all. For all her trappings of power, her sun-streaked hair, the golden *G* on her shoulder and hip, she was nothing. I realized that I was the dangerous one. I was the dragon. I could feel all of Wayburn Woods spread out behind me, blazing in the fire of an autumn sun, a great green dragon with spiked trees along its sprawling back, and a languid blue lake for a tail.

"You seem so interested in Rachel's food. I certainly

understand; she's a wonderful cook. You really should come see our cabin, or 'fort,' as you call it. Sample some of Rachel's forest cuisine. Do you think they could find it, Rachel? I suppose we could leave a trail of crumbs for you to follow. Maybe even acorn crumbs." I smiled and laced up my shoes.

Cindy's eyes again bore into me. "Thank you so much. I'm sure we would just love to come to your hut sometime and join your little club for freaks." They left the locker room laughing. I pulled Rachel's head out of the locker and hurried her into her uniform so we wouldn't be late for field hockey lineups.

Rachel was such an accomplished person: she could use an electric drill, she could read almost any book in two days, she could make chili and biscuits for a family of fifteen. I could place Rachel into any chapter of my American history book. She could have churned butter and carded wool in a New England colony. She could have farmed the expanses of the Kansas Territory, traveled the Oregon Trail. She could have nursed an entire wagon train through a smallpox epidemic, founded a town, and run a telegraph office, but she didn't have what counted most in school. Her eyes were small, intelligent, observant, and her nose turned upward. She had a solid square shape, not fat, but rock hard and sturdy. Rachel didn't have the kind of attractiveness that was easy to see. And *that* was an injustice, though not one you could write an editorial about in the *Pine Press*.

By the end of eighth period she had recovered in the cool air of the playing fields. Ms. Estuary, our P.E. teacher, let us practice passing shots all period, so we stayed near the line of trees, away from the frenzy of the Friday playoffs in which Cindy Wedford featured heavily. After smacking the ball past me a few times, Rachel said, "I think you should come over after school. We need to discuss some things."

"Rachel, if you're worried about Cindy . . ."

"No, no. That was no big deal. I want to talk about the cabin. It needs to be winterized. My dad has some ideas about making it weatherproof. If we don't, the boards are going to warp and rot and by this spring it will need major work. I think you should come over and stay the night so we can make plans."

I was pretty certain that Rachel had never asked another human being to be an overnight guest, and the honor of it was not lost on me.

"Sure. I'd like to come," I said.

"Good. We eat about six, and we're having spaghetti. So don't be late or there won't be any left."

Mr. McDuff had another dazzling evening planned for my mother. They were going to the Skyline for cocktails, the Parthenon for dinner, then the Fielding Theatre for a stage show. While I packed an overnight bag, Mother swished around in a taffeta slip, rejecting dresses, trying out earrings, spraying the air with perfume and hair spray. Mr. McDuff arrived in a black suit and handed Mother a long gold box filled with red roses.

"Oh, they're long-stemmed! How lovely, Louis. A dozen perfect roses!"

"Two dozen," he said softly.

She clicked away in her high heels to put them in water, and I waited with Mr. McDuff in the entry.

"And someone told me that you have a weakness for chocolate milk shakes." From somewhere he produced a white bag from Blitz Burger. Inside was a jumbo shake, straw and all.

"Thank you," I said, not knowing if I should start in on it or just hold on to the bag. "And I'm sure enjoying the book, Mr. McDuff."

"The book?"

"The book about Walden Pond."

"Oh, yes. So you're reading it, are you?" He sounded surprised.

"I'm at the chapter called 'Sounds.' Henry talks a lot about the train whistle in the distance and the birds that he heard at night."

"Well, that's just fine, Beth," he said. He wasn't really interested in the sounds of Walden Pond, and I don't know why I persisted in repeating them just then.

"One of the birds, a screech owl, sounded like it was saying, *'Oh-o-o-o-o that I never had been bor-r-r-r-n!'*"

He shook his head. "Is that right?"

My mother returned wearing a silk stole and clutching a sequined purse. Mr. McDuff lost his slight interest in the owls when he saw her, and they talked in low tones until he pulled his Mercedes into the driveway of the Haygen house.

Two bedraggled skeletons from Halloween still dangled from the front doors. My mother leaned across the seat and kissed me. "Have a wonderful time, darling. Call me tomorrow and I'll pick you up."

I crunched through dead leaves to the porch steps, though before I could knock, two sentries opened it for me.

"She's here!" one of them shouted. And it seemed that a whirlwind of activity began in every corner of the house. The other boy studied the Blitz bag I was still holding.

"I'm Stephen," he said, not taking his eyes off it.

Rachel came sliding around the corner in her socks, a splash of red sauce down the front of her blouse. I handed her the bag.

"I brought you something. Do you like chocolate?"

"Thanks." She glanced at her younger brothers as if to say, I told you she was worth waiting for!

The occasion of Rachel's first overnight guest was taken seriously by the Haygen clan. I became their reigning queen as I stepped over a dollhouse and a barnyard of plastic animals. Every Haygen was presented to me for introduction: Stephen and Michael, the two door guards; then a whole crowd of them under ten years old: Mary, Anna, Matt, and Grace—there were so many, I lost count. Thomas and Kenneth, upperclassmen at school, drifted in and introduced themselves. A quiet older sister, Sylvia, glided by. Paul and Ryan, fifteen and sixteen respectively, waved at me with Ping-Pong paddles.

All were friendly and inquisitive, and all were in stocking feet, slipping and skidding on the hardwood. I learned that socks were the Haygens' mode of transportation about that barn of a house. That explained why the oak floors were so polished: legions of soft, tireless feet buffed them every day. Stephen and Michael actually skated down the hall to check on the garlic bread, swinging their arms to the sides, torsos bent forward, heads low. Anchored by clodhoppers, I felt like a clumsy barge in the midst of a hundred speeding skiffs.

Mrs. Haygen, a petite woman with glasses, greeted me warmly and led me by the hand to the dining room. Mr. Haygen couldn't join us, much to his regret. A power line in Rockroad Harbor was down.

"My dad works for the Crestview Power Company," Stephen said. "He goes to emergencies and fixes people's electricity."

"He's a dispatcher and manages the transformer crews," Kenneth said.

Stephen was unabashed by this correction. "Sometimes he's gone all night. Like last year in the ice storm, Dad was gone a whole week."

"I remember that," I said. "My mom and I lost our power for days and had to use candles."

"My dad fixed the wires for you," Stephen answered. Kenneth sighed.

"Well, he did!" cried Stephen.

The Haygen children showed remarkable control that night at the dinner table. Small hands impulsively sprang out to grab passing bowls of salad and garlic bread but were slapped down by older hands. When Anna rose from her seat to reach for the can of Parmesan cheese about four feet away, Paul hauled her back in place by the collar. In fact, whenever anyone reached for anything, a dozen pairs of eyes reminded him by a jerk of the head to look in my direction first. I had to grab mouthfuls in between a barrage of polite offers.

"Would you like some more s'ghetti?" Grace asked after she had served herself.

"You want some milk too?" Stephen asked in the middle of pouring his own.

Stephen evidently felt he had found someone who shared his devotion for his father, Hugh Haygen, and he followed us around after dinner, coasting silently on blue socks. He stayed just out of Rachel's reach and close enough to be of service to me. Like a grim-faced little butler, he anticipated when I might need a hand towel or a glass of water, or would I like to try a new paddle against Matt's spin serve?

Ping-Pong was the winter sport at the Haygen house after the sun went down. Naturally, they played shoeless, and they had invented all sorts of tricks. The younger children were just as skilled as the older ones and were in great demand for their piggyback version of Ping-Pong. Grace and Matt would ride Ryan and Rachel so that they could return high lobs off the ceiling. Their "donkeys" would slam net-skimming drives across the table. Spectators sat on stacks of clean laundry around the table, cheering, and when a "piggy" scraped plaster from the ceiling with his paddle, they went berserk. Then came the round-about games where players ran around the table and could return the ball only while they were sliding. The older boys had refined the slides to include twirls in the air and one-footed landings. Mrs. Haygen would walk in occasionally to see if anyone was bleeding and then disappear again to a distant room on the first floor.

When we finally began the climb to Rachel's third-floor room, I was worn out. At the second floor the landing opened up onto a large sitting room, where books and magazines lay in heaps. An old man sat slumped over, a cup and saucer in his lap.

"My grandfather," Rachel said. "That's how he sleeps."

We climbed the narrower third-story stairs and Stephen followed, dragging my suitcase and placing it on a top bunk in Rachel's room.

"Is she going to sleep on the upper, Rache?" he asked.

"Just get lost," she said.

Unlike the rest of the house, Rachel's room was orderly and calm. She had furnished it herself from the warehouse of Haygen antiques. She had a rolltop desk from the garage apartment, a Victorian love seat from the attic, an ornate floor lamp, and an entire wall of books. She organized them by preference: her favorites were on the top shelves near the window and from there they descended in value and spread across the shelves until the nearly worthless titles were in a crate by the door.

There were no childhood souvenirs, no stuffed animals, no china horses. Take away the bunk bed and it could have been an office. I liked it, though. The banter and nonstop roughhousing of the Haygen children couldn't reach us here, and I was grateful for the break.

"The cabin needs shingles," she said from the bottom bunk. "Don't worry, my dad has thousands of them. We'll nail them onto the outside walls and they'll not only block out wind, they'll also deflect rain and snow."

I leaned over the side of my bunk. Rachel's plaid flannel pajamas made her look like a lumberjack. She was propped up on one elbow and still wore her glasses.

"Then we'll plaster the inside to seal up the cracks and seams." She talked on, but I was thinking of the honeycomb of her house and how different it was to be sleeping in a building where eleven other children were stashed away in rooms and niches I hadn't even seen. A few times I heard the muffled thump of stocking feet in a final glide to a bathroom, but otherwise the household quieted and slept. Mrs. Haygen was still up, I think, reading by a lamp on the first floor, waiting for Mr. Haygen, who was out there somewhere in the night, saving people from the darkness.

Chapter 8

"To affect the quality of the day,
that is the highest of arts."
H. D. THOREAU

As we were only on chapter six of *Walden,* I had no idea that Henry had plastered his cabin when the cold weather came. Rachel knew about it, though, because she'd read all the way up to chapter thirteen, called "House-Warming." On Saturday morning she was ready with sand and limestone, buckets and trowels, a wagonload of shingles, and, most important, Mr. Haygen. He was energetic and showed no sign that he had been up most of the night dispatching crews of linemen. We loaded our supplies on the flatbed behind his tractor and rode to the edge of Wayburn.

Mr. Haygen started nailing the shingles to the north side of the cabin. He whacked them into the horizontal boards and moved up in even rows. He could drive a nail through with one blow of his hammer and soon had half the wall covered. Then he handed over the hammer and made me try. I bent every nail on the first stroke, but he patiently pulled each one out.

"You've got to be more confident with a hammer," he told me. "Fix your sight on the shingle, not the nail head. There you go." He coached me until before I knew it, I was pounding in the top row.

Rachel and I worked our way around the cabin while Mr. Haygen cut a two-foot opening on the west wall and installed a four-paned window that swung out on hinges to let air in. After Mr. Haygen left, we used trowels to plaster the cracks between the boards and in every chink and knothole that might admit cold air.

If I had read chapter thirteen, I would also have known that Henry felt just like I did. He said, "My house never pleased my eye so much after it was plastered." Instead of the rough and knotty walls, we now had civilized-looking white seams between the planks, though the ceiling and floor, like Henry's, were still solid wood.

"Listen, you can't hear the wind," I whispered to Rachel.

"Even better, you can't feel it," she said.

"It's a real house now, a house in the woods."

"Most definitely it is." She smoothed a lump of plaster and tossed her trowel into the bucket. "By the time we go get our gear and gather some firewood, it'll be set up enough."

"Enough for what?"

"Enough to sleep here. We'll just be careful." She touched up a small hole under the window frame with her thumb.

"You're serious?"

"What's the point of a house in the woods if you can't sleep in it? Henry lived in his for two years!"

With only an hour to sundown, we had to be efficient. As we flew down the path to Middleton Road, strong winds from the lake roared up into the treetops, shaking leaves down around us as we ran. My legs pounded the path and a giddy exhilaration pounded in my chest. Wayburn Woods trembled and shimmied, as if rehearsing for winter nights to come.

We arrived panting at the Haygen house, shouting orders to each other. Rachel had the longer list: sleeping bags, blankets, flashlight, and food for at least a day, maybe more. We were reeling with sudden opportunity. Who knew how long we might stay!

I was to call my mother and get an extension to my sleepover, and there I unexpectedly hit a brick wall. It seemed that Mr. McDuff had planned an evening that included me. He was bringing over Chinese food and had envisioned us playing cards and watching television. A few uncertain moments passed when my mother's fear of disappointing him almost won out; that is, until I reminded her that Rachel and I were still at work on our school project. I hung up with a nagging mental picture of Mr. McDuff growing ever larger in our entry hall.

Rachel was gesturing impatiently outside the window. "We still have to get firewood!" she yelled. Most of our supplies were stuffed into backpacks and faithful Stephen was holding them in the driveway.

The wind whipped around us wildly. By the time we reached the three-tiered hill it was dark, and we found the trail by flashlight. We threw our packs inside the cabin and scavenged the edges of the Old Grove for dry kindling.

We pulled the parlor chairs close to the fire, roasted hot dogs in the stove, and listened to the racket outside. Wind battered the branches overhead and wailed around the submarine tree.

Later, the moon climbed higher and beat on our door with its brightness. We started down to the lake with a bucket but stopped at the edge of the slope. Moonlight had draped Wayburn in dark green velvet, black satin skirts. Jewelry sparkled below the lake's surface as if in the depths a party swirled, and we realized that Wayburn Woods led a secret nightlife. By day she was frank and green, but by night she was nothing but refined, silky mystery.

"Look," Rachel whispered. "The moonlight comes down in shafts, just like the sunlight." She was right. In the Old Grove pale silver beams shot down through the canopy of white oaks.

"Like a fairyland," I said.

"Like Lothlorien in Middle Earth," Rachel replied.

"We could hike by moonlight if we followed the shore-line."

"Tonight we could do anything!"

We hoisted a bucket of water up from the lake for washing. We put our heaviest wood in the stove. We pushed the furniture aside and spread our sleeping bags in front of the fire, but we were too wind-tossed to sleep. We sat in the doorway, facing the darkness. Finally we ran laughing into the Old Grove, over the glowing moss, through showers of moonbeams.

Later, when clouds moved in and the wind chilled, we went inside and stirred up the flames in the stove.

"Could you live like this, Rachel? I mean, all the time, by yourself, like Henry did?"

"Yes. I'd love to get away from the mob in my house," she said.

"But to be completely alone . . . on a night like tonight say, when there would be no one to share it with." She thought for a while and didn't answer.

"I don't know if I could," I said. "That's the part of the experiment we didn't try."

I pictured Henry moving around our cabin, writing in his journal, staring at the fire, night after night. I imagined the scratch of his pen, the creak of a chair leg, the soft snapping of the fire. I blinked the image away and suddenly it was our cabin again.

"Beth," Rachel said quietly from her sleeping bag, "how did Cindy and those girls know about my acorns?"

"Stuart," I said. "It had to be him."

"Of course." She took off her glasses and rubbed her eyes. "I should have known that."

"I'm sure he didn't mean for it to turn out the way it did. You know Stuart, he was probably bragging to them about our projects, how we're more in tune with the spirit of Henry than anyone else."

"I'm not so sure," she said. "He's a reporter now, and reporters can't be trusted. They're always looking for a good story."

"Stuart's not mean, though, not like Cindy and her friends."

"He can really get on my nerves sometimes," Rachel said. "Like the way he reads to us as if he's some professor or something. When I think of that contract—what nerve! He made us sign it and now he doesn't even believe in it anymore. Now he's off on that civil disobedience nonsense. And his map isn't all that great. He acts as if he invented Wayburn Woods."

"He did lead us out here."

"Oh, that's another thing. Do you know he once told me that he could have been another Meriwether Lewis, except that he'd been born in the wrong century? He is so conceited!"

"Not conceited, confident."

"Stop defending him! We would have found Wayburn eventually, even without Stuart, the famous explorer."

"Anyway, it's almost over. Presentations start soon."

"Yes, but watch what you say around him. Remember, we have a spy in our midst."

I thought Rachel was being overly suspicious, but then, I wasn't the one who'd been attacked by a dragon because of Stuart's carelessness.

The fire sank into embers and we fell asleep in Wayburn Woods. I wondered what creatures roamed around the cabin that night, sniffing at our camp, scampering past the door, and throwing their shadows against our shingled walls.

When I woke, the fire was out, and though it was warm inside my covers, my breath was puffing out in white clouds. I also knew we weren't alone. Something was breathing faintly outside the cabin.

"Rachel, there's something outside. Listen!" I said. She fumbled for her glasses as if they would help her hear better.

"It's probably Stephen and Michael." She sighed. "Only they'd be imbecilic enough to come out here at the crack of dawn."

We heard more movement outside, the barest crunch of leaves.

"That's not Stephen and Michael," I whispered fiercely. "I can feel a whole bunch of them, a crowd of something!"

Rachel sat up. "Well, what, then? Mrs. Stark's class?" She cleaned her glasses with the lining of her sleeping bag. "I'm going to look," she said. Someone knocked lightly on the door. A thin voice spoke into the doorjamb.

"Beth, Rachel, come out, but be really quiet."

"Hollis!" we said together. We dressed quickly and eased the door open to see that beyond the door, beyond Hollis, was a gathering of brown-and-black shapes. Black heads and beaks turned in unison to face us: Canada geese, acres of them it seemed, from the shoreline up the slope, scattered throughout the forest edges, up to within a few feet of the cabin.

"What do they want?" I asked.

"Food," Rachel said. "They're on their way south for the winter. They fly over Hawthorn Lake every fall, but never so many."

"Thousands," Hollis whispered. "Thousands."

Rachel backed toward the cabin and every bird in the front row stiffened. A few rocked back and forth on leathery brown legs, but they waited while she retrieved a box of cereal. She knelt down and placed her hand on the ground. From several rows back one of the geese edged closer and pecked the flakes from her palm. Slowly, the enormous tableau came to life and the geese moved forward.

When the cereal was gone we fed them bread, cornmeal, stale cookies, and Stuart's cracked corn, which was their favorite and brought more geese waddling up the hillside. Rachel's pantry finally gave out, though, and we could offer only our empty hands. We never saw which goose gave the signal, but every bird suddenly turned and headed for the lake. They slid into the inlet below the cabin and floated away as silently as they had come.

"Did you see that?" Hollis kept asking us. "Did you see that?"

"We saw it, Hollis," Rachel answered.

"They were like the flying monkeys in *The Wizard of Oz*. Before you came out I saw them land. The sky was black with their wings. Why do you think they picked our beach? Can you explain that? Just like the flying monkeys!"

"At least they didn't carry us away," Rachel said.

"We've got to follow them!"

"How?" Rachel asked. "They're swimming to who-knows-where, and if you get close, they'll just fly away."

"They might not—then again—I wonder if they might come back," he wondered aloud.

"I doubt it. They're migrating south, but maybe others will stop. I don't know!" Rachel said irritably. The magic of last night's wind and moon had been deflated by the morning's hard, sharp facts: we had no kindling and geese had eaten our breakfast.

"Well, I'm going after them. It's too coincidental the way they came here to us. It may be a sign; they may be trying to . . . tell us something."

"And what would they want to tell us?" Rachel asked, exasperated.

"I'm not sure," Hollis said, "but the one who walked up first, he reminded me of Gort."

"Good grief," Rachel said, and she began picking up small sticks and bundling them into her sweatshirt.

"Who's Gort?" I asked.

86

"*The Day the Earth Stood Still*—it's a movie. Gort was the robot who came to patrol the earth. After his spaceship landed, he just stood outside the door and wouldn't move."

"Don't you ever see any *modern* movies, the kind most people see?" Rachel said.

Hollis continued. "All the scientists in the world tried to get him to move and they couldn't. You had to know the special words."

"Don't tell me!" Rachel called out from behind the cabin.

"Klaatu, the spaceman, sent the lady from Earth to give Gort a message. She had to get the message right or Gort would disintegrate the entire world. I memorized it too; you never know when you might need something like that."

I could see Rachel peering around the side of the cabin, too fed up to come out but too intrigued not to listen.

"And what was the message?" I asked.

Hollis had calmed down. He took a long time forming his words, as if the survival of the world depended on his accuracy. He said: *"Gort, Klaatu barata nikto."*

Rachel shook her head.

"What does it mean?" I said.

"I don't know exactly," he began, "but Gort closed his flap and didn't destroy the earth; instead, he took the lady to the spaceship, where she'd be safe."

"Let me see if I understand," Rachel said, setting down a bunch of sticks inside the cabin. "You want to find the geese and give them that message."

87

"No, that's not what I meant. Forget it, I'll go myself." Hollis started down the slope, looking so slight and rumpled that I had to follow him. Rachel came too.

"Hollis, how will you find them? They're probably in the middle of the lake by now," I said.

"I have a canoe," he said, pointing to the inlet, where a green canoe was half hidden in the reeds.

"Since when have you had a canoe?" Rachel demanded.

Hollis shrugged. "We've always had it. My brother and I patched up the holes yesterday and carried it over this morning. Look, I'll see you later."

We all ended up in the canoe, which sprang a new leak, so that one of us had to bail continuously with a tin can. We finally spotted the geese cruising around the L-shaped turn in the lake, and because the message was so important to Hollis, it became important to us too.

We had never seen all of Wayburn Lake. As we rounded the bend, the lake became oval, thickly wooded up to its edges. No rafts, no docks, no motorboats or catamarans, only far off to the south, the spire of Our Lady of the Hills Chapel jutted over the treetops.

Hollis and I maintained our pace. We followed the stragglers and relied on their soft honking to guide us. They led us to what seemed the end of the world, up to a weedy corner of the lake, where lily pads covered the surface. Some Wayburn dairy cows were grazing at the shoreline. My arms were spent; my lungs ached. We drifted, resting while the geese held a sort of conference in the lily pads.

They gave us no warning before they left. They simply rose up in a roar of flapping, slapping, and honking. They lifted from the water, rising over the cows, over the steeple of Our Lady of the Hills Chapel, and banked to the south in a long, scrawling line. Then they were nothing but a jagged rupture in the sky.

Hollis sat in the bow, more absorbed than if he had seen a spaceship ascend. Rachel and I agreed later that when the geese flew off that morning, part of Hollis flew off too. We never again heard him refer to movies after that, as if he had finally witnessed something that had no parallel in film. But when the distant honking died out, we heard an awkward, ugly sound: the slap of a single wing on water.

Out across the lily pads a solitary goose jerked and twisted in the weeds, desperate to follow.

"There it is," he said. "That's the message."

Hollis leaned out over the bow and paddled with deep alternating strokes toward the huddled shape. I bore down on my left side, reaching down so far, the weeds slithered across my wrists. I strained to give him all the speed I could, but it was like rowing along a jungle path. Rachel bailed frantically to free us of the water we'd taken on while watching the geese fly off. Sometimes the lily pads disappeared, and we skimmed over tall, ropy plants waving in the deep waters beneath us. All the while we headed for the goose, I felt we were creeping into a stagnant, marshy trap.

We drew close enough to see that it was hopelessly snared in a minnow net. I was starting to feel sickened by the whole mess: the rank, weedy smell, the ever-thicker lily pads, and the hoarse honking of the dying goose. We pulled the canoe up beside it, and Hollis slipped out of his shoes and stepped over the side of the canoe, his windbreaker billowing out behind him on the water.

"At least take your jacket off, you idiot," Rachel yelled.

He wriggled out of it and threw it into the canoe.

"Are you sure you should be doing this?" I asked him.

"It is pretty cold," he sputtered, and smiled crookedly at us. He pushed the weeds aside and was within reach of the goose. You could tell that the goose saw Hollis as an extension of the net, possibly the *maker* of the net, and he flailed his free wing so violently that Hollis ducked his head under the water.

"He's strong!" he cried, breaking the surface.

Hollis tried to swim around to the pinned wing, but the goose turned, keeping his open wing between them.

Rachel and I paddled closer, thinking we could hoist the two of them into the canoe, but the bird flogged his free wing pitifully against the canoe as if it were yet another threat. His brown and black feathers heaved and trembled underneath the net; his head was coiled under; his smooth black eye was glassed over with fear.

I didn't actually think about jumping into the lake. I just found myself sliding into the icy water, into the thick weeds next to Hollis.

"Are you sure you should be doing this?" he asked.

"I've got an idea," I said. "I'll hold his good wing against his body, and then you work the net off."

I swam up to the free wing, and when the goose opened it to trounce me, I grabbed the end of it, put my face down into the water, and kicked until it folded. I slipped one arm over its back and the other around its breast and buried my face in its feathers. The bird bit at my arms and shoulders and thrust a leg into my chest.

Hollis was tattered and scratched but managed to keep the net from tearing into the goose's shoulder any more than it had. He stretched out the wing and gently untangled the feathers along its trailing edge.

That goose must have hated me, saddled to its back, my hot human breath in its feathers. It struggled more sporadically and made shallow rasping sounds. Then Hollis held up a torn section of net and backed away.

"It's off," he said. "Except for the foot, it's off."

I released my grip and backed off too. The black head arched from side to side, taking stock of the damage we had done, and for a minute the goose swam around in the shredded leaves between us. Hollis reached up and ran his hand down its back, and to my lifelong amazement the goose allowed it. But before Hollis could touch it again, it spread its wings and sprang across the water, using the lily pads as a runway. The minnow net dangled from one webbed toe.

Hollis cried out and dove after it.

"Forget the net!" Rachel shouted. "It'll drop!"

The goose strained upward, tucking in its feet like landing gear, and the net fell away. It cut swiftly into the air and aimed for the same trees its companions had topped. Within moments it was a tiny black **V** disappearing into grayness.

Hollis wouldn't get into the canoe until he had found the net, though his lips were blue and his teeth were clicking uncontrollably. He held on to the side while Rachel and I paddled along the goose's flight path. Luckily we spotted the net on the surface, buoyed up by plants, or Hollis would have never rested.

"The next victim might have been a muskrat or a snapping turtle," he said. "They should outlaw minnow nets."

Later we hung the net in the cabin. Hollis called it Gort's Trophy. He thought it gave the cabin atmosphere, like those seafood restaurants in Rockroad Harbor. But maybe displaying the minnow net was not such a good idea, because Hollis was never the same after he rescued Gort from the noose. He began to fear for all the birds. He thought the sparrows looked too thin, and the mallards were much too trusting of humans. He forgot all about the insects and began protecting the birds of Wayburn Woods. And though he worried in general about the birds, he worried in particular about Gort.

"Do you think he found the others?" he often asked us.

Rachel and I took care to be convincing. "Of course he did. Canada geese have standard migration paths. I'm sure he picked right up on their trail," she'd answer.

"You don't think he was too tired after all that struggling in the water?"

"Not at all. He took off like a shot. I could even feel the draft from his wings!" I'd say, and Hollis would believe me because I had been in the water beside him.

Still, after that day, he watched the sky, the water, and the shoreline for Gort and for all those that flew.

Chapter 9

"I have, as it were, my own sun and moon and stars,
and a little world all to myself."

H. D. Thoreau

The current issue of the *Pine Press* always turned up in Wayburn Woods. Rachel, Hollis, and I might have been somewhat removed from the events of school, but we were not out of touch. We had become fairly regular in our habits at the cabin too. The days were getting shorter, leaving us only a couple of hours of daylight on the weekdays. I got off at Rachel's bus stop nearly every day after school, and we went directly to the woods.

We had our own study hall in the twilight hours before dark. Hollis would pretend to work for about ten minutes, then he would stand and say, "I think I'd better go check the feeders, see if the sparrows like the new seed blend." He would traipse around the forest like a trapper checking his lines, except Hollis's traps were garbage-can lids that he had tied to tree limbs. He'd climb up, peer in the trays, and be thrilled when he found them empty.

Rachel never had any homework. She always finished it before she left school, and she always had an explanation. "I waited twenty minutes to use the iron in my sewing class. What was I supposed to do?"

I was the only one who did homework; at least I tried to with Rachel reading aloud sections of the *Press* she found especially irksome. She was tolerant of the feature journalists who wrote the front-page news, but on Stuart's editorials she was brutal.

"Listen to this," she said, pushing her glasses into place.

"I can't find prepositional phrases if you read that, Rachel."

So she read silently but carried on a running debate with Stuart over his ideas. "Oh really? And what makes you think we'd want Friday fun nights in the auditorium, Stuart? Not all of us 'inmates' are feeling so mistreated by Pine Brook Prison that we need to bounce on trampolines and swing from the parallel bars while some D.J. plays music. Maybe some of us have a different concept of fun."

"Do you know what Stuart's problem is?" she said after a brief silence. "Well, I'll tell you. He wants to run the world. That's why he started this newspaper. Out here he had only the three of us to boss around; now he's got the whole school. But just watch, even that won't be enough. And don't kid yourself—it's not civil disobedience he's after; it's obedience to Stuart."

She turned back to the front page and wagged her head sadly. "These poor feature journalists. Don't they realize they're being used? We're all being used, *forced* to write articles for this paper—I'll bet it violates some kind of child labor laws."

None of my articles had been selected for publication in the *Press,* and personally I didn't care. Dinner at Blitz's was no lure for me; our freezer at home was lined with frozen milk shakes, Mr. McDuff's calling cards whenever he came to take my mother out on a date. He often took me to Blitz's when Mother went to her real estate class.

"You can go to the best restaurant in town," he said respectfully, "but you can't beat this burger." I never saw Mr. McDuff in anything but a suit; he would eat two Blitz burgers, leaning way over, almost parallel to the tabletop, so that the juices wouldn't drip on him. The bald spot on his head would glow in the neon pulse of the Blitz's sign. Sometimes I would bring the *Press* with us, and Mr. McDuff and I would read it while we ate.

"This Stuart fellow writes a decent article, docsn't he?" Mr. McDuff said.

"I guess. He gets carried away, though, and makes school sound worse than it is."

"Then why don't you submit an opinion? Give him a run for his money. Nothing stimulates a newspaper like a little competition." He winked encouragingly at me.

But I had nothing to say about school, and just to show my indifference, I wrapped up my extra french fries in the editorial page. In class I wrote feature articles as Mrs. Stark assigned them, but I stubbornly ignored her guidance concerning topics.

"What major events have occurred this past week about which we might write articles?" she asked in class every Friday. While most kids wrote about the student council bake sale, the chorus assembly, or junior varsity basketball tryouts, I wrote about the rescue of Gort.

Aside from Rachel's ongoing criticism of the *Press*, the events at school didn't affect our lives in Wayburn Woods. We lived in another country, in another century, and we lived for the weekends when we could spend whole days in the woods. By the middle of November temperatures were dropping to freezing, and even the afternoons remained cloudy and cold. When we saw the first snow flurries, we stacked extra wood behind the cabin and covered it with a tarp.

Rachel stayed inside the cabin reading and tending the woodstove most of the time, though she still foraged for edible plants and checked off the ones in her field guide that she had found. On Saturday she searched all morning and came back with a bucket full of chickweed and chufa plants; then she spent the afternoon chopping and boiling her finds. But we didn't worry too much about eating like Henry anymore.

"Times have changed," Rachel explained. "If Thoreau were around today, he'd eat convenience foods too, so he could spend more time outside."

That sounded reasonable to me, and our meals became a mix of Rachel's original forest cuisine and whatever we could pilfer from home; nothing fancy: cans of soup, bread, peanut butter. Occasionally Stephen was allowed to haul out a supply wagon, and I paid him back with frozen milk shakes. Rachel always had something hot on the stove for us when we came in from the cold.

"She's like one of those perfect housewives from the nineteen fifties," Hollis said.

"Right," I added. "All she needs is an apron, and she could meet us at the door, smiling."

"I can live without the apron, but the smiling part sounds like a nice change," he said.

"Shut up," Rachel answered, pouring him some tomato soup.

"What are these green things?" he asked.

"Miner's lettuce. I found it in the Old Grove. It was sheltered from the wind, that's why it's still around."

"I thought we were going to eat normal food," Hollis said.

"This is as normal as you are. Besides, it's rich in vitamin A, which is good for your eyes. Eat this and you'll be able to spot a wood thrush eating a sesame seed at fifty yards."

Hollis would have eaten silt from the lake bottom if he thought it would further his bird quest. Rachel knew this, and as much as she teased him, she encouraged his study of the birds.

She brought him a field guide of North American birds

from home, and he disappeared with it all day Sunday. Mr. Haygen gave him some old military binoculars. They looked painfully heavy around Hollis's slender neck. He took to toting around a sketch pad as well. Yet with all this baggage, Hollis was never burdened. He vaulted over thickets, scooted under fallen branches, and straddled limbs to catch birds in his view.

After a good sighting he'd sketch the bird from memory, wherever he happened to be, consult the field guide, make corrections, and then draw it again. He called his collection "The Ones Who Stayed Behind—A Survey of Winter Birds in Wayburn Woods." Later, he tinted the sketches with colored pencils and labeled them in his simple printing: "*Melospiza melodia:* Song Sparrow." He hung a chart in the cabin, listing the birds he'd seen along with a thumbnail sketch and the location of the sighting:

European Starling
Sturnus vulgaris
Nov. 15, about 3:00 P.M.
I saw him in the big tree above the canoe landing.
He was probably looking for some dinner
in the cattail marsh.

Next to the chart he wrote down his goals for the week, names like white-breasted nuthatch, horned lark, or downy woodpecker—the birds he wanted to see and sketch.

I wrote every day in my journal. Rachel and Hollis

never read it, but I did sift out the most interesting tidbit each week to submit to Mrs. Stark as my feature article. I recorded all the events of our life in the woods: Hollis's sighting of the great horned owl, Rachel's discovery of a goosefoot plant, and the first ice I found in the inlet on Sunday morning.

On Monday the long-awaited Presentation Week finally arrived. I can only imagine the nightmare it must have been for Brendan Fain. He was the first presenter, the first human sacrifice to walk to the podium. I felt particularly bad for him because I had so often dodged behind him when Mrs. Stark went looking for oral readers. He showed us a poster he'd made of a man lying under a tree. Brendan's absent partner was supposed to have read from *Walden,* and together they were going to add commentary. Now that he was alone, Brendan chickened out. He just stood there curling and uncurling his poster so that all we saw consistently were Henry's feet.

Thankfully Mrs. Stark cut Brendan's suffering short. "What a shame your partner, Jimmy, couldn't be here today. I'm sure his dramatic reading would have rounded out your presentation nicely. And what original artwork!" Brendan stumbled gratefully back to his seat. I reached out and patted the huge shoulder that had bulged over the rim of my desktop since September, but Brendan was so shell-shocked, he didn't feel it.

Next came a peppy little tour called "Walden and the Concord Environs" by Janice Phelson and Marjorie Winfred. They alternately described points of interest around Walden

Pond and suggested how we might apply Mr. Thoreau's wisdom to our own lives. They were really quite polished and reminded me of miniatures of those flight attendants who point out the exit doors and the oxygen masks above your airplane seat.

"In our experiment, we found that Mr. Thoreau's example can be a real lifesaver," Janice said.

Marjorie nodded. "So the next time you feel desperate and overly rushed, stop to enjoy the beauty of nature all around you."

"That's right. And now we'd like to end with this final quote of Mr. Thoreau's," Janice said. "'Our life is frittered away by detail. An honest man has hardly need to count more than his ten fingers, or in extreme cases he may add his ten toes, and lump the rest. Simplicity, simplicity, simplicity!'"

The curtain rose and fell again on Tuesday and Wednesday. Group after group came forward to pay homage to Henry and to show how he'd changed their lives. Many poems were read about sitting next to streams and listening to birds sing. I discovered I wasn't the only one keeping a diary. Countless journals were displayed with paper flowers on the cover or pictures cut out from *National Geographic*.

Jake Spenner wrote a one-act play called "The Untold Truth of My Stay at Walden." Jake played the part of Henry and wore a secondhand tuxedo he'd found. The play was a monologue in which Henry confessed that cravings for meat pies and bread pudding drove him into town each night, where he resorted to stealing to satisfy his hunger. Jake clutched his hair and paced the stage in agitation. I thought it was a silly and unflattering way to portray Henry, and that it had more to do with *The Wolf Man* than *Walden*. The class loved it.

Many maps were unfurled, though none as magnificent as Stuart's. Long passages of Henry's were read from stiff, colorless faces whose eyes never looked up and whose voices soothed us into sleepiness. When the last group on Wednesday strung a sheet between two desks and announced a puppet show, "Henry's Summer Morning," we were almost delirious with excitement. Jerry Jacobs and Richard Lowell had cleverly based their script on a sentence from the chapter called "Sounds."

"Sometimes, in a summer morning—"

After a long pause a paper sun rose up shakily over the sheet.

". . . having taken my accustomed bath—"

Another lengthy silence and then we heard hands splashing in a bowl behind the curtain.

". . . I sat in my sunny doorway from sunrise till noon, rapt in a revery . . ."

At last Henry appeared. No one minded that he was a paper doll taped to a ruler. And even when Jerry and Richard whispered anxiously to each other between spoken lines, no one minded that either. We were giving the puppeteers lots of leeway.

". . . amidst the pines and hickories and sumachs, in undisturbed solitude and stillness—"

Trees eventually sprang up behind Henry, but evidently their order was in dispute backstage. When the sumac popped up before the pines, Jerry snatched it back down and there were more tense whispers. The audience started filling in the empty stage time with their own sighs and sound effects.

"... *while the birds sang around or flitted noiseless through the house* ..."

Things picked up a little here, but mostly because the birds that swooped across the stage on clothes-hanger wire were as big as Henry and had evil-looking eyes.

Following Mrs. Stark's cue, we applauded every presentation. And we clapped most loudly for the last performance of the day, no matter how tedious it had been. Our motives were mixed. We clapped out of relief, out of pity for our classmates, and out of gratitude that we still had days to go before it was our turn.

At the cabin we were doing our best not to think about Friday. But on Wednesday afternoon we had an unpleasant reminder. As Rachel was shelling acorns she noticed footsteps outside the cabin. Hollis was adding the ruffed grouse to his bird chart, when they both heard voices on the old path, the one we hardly used anymore. I was bringing up a jug of cider from the lake when I saw Stuart and Kathy Dulack stroll into the clearing.

Stuart was pointing out things, shaking his head in wonderment as if he were returning to a scene from his childhood.

"It's just like your map, Stu," Kathy said.

"Beth!" He turned to face me.

"Hello," I said. Stuart looked older, in a way that newspaper deadlines and budget deals with the class treasurer make you look older. Kathy wore a suede jacket over what I assumed was a complete Glamma outfit for walking in the woods.

"You've really done a lot to the cabin," he said, touching the shingles.

"We winterized it," I said.

"You still spend a lot of time here?"

I could see he felt sorry for me, as if there was something pathetic about spending time in Wayburn Woods.

"I guess we do. What's wrong with that?"

"Nothing. It's just . . . I don't know. It seems strange to still be doing the Experiment in Living now that it's all over."

Honestly, I had forgotten about the Experiment in Living. We hadn't called it that for weeks now. I didn't know how to tell Stuart that the experiment he remembered so distantly had become our lives. I couldn't explain that, not with him studying me like I was a social misfit and Kathy brushing dirt off the tops of her shoes.

Just then Rachel opened the cabin door. She stood in the doorway, wiping her hands on a dish towel she had wrapped around her waist. At the moment, she didn't look at all like a perfect fifties housewife.

"I'm going down for some acorn meal," she announced.

"The coffee will be ready in half an hour." She walked down the slope to the lake, where she had a gunnysack full of crushed acorns inside a bushel basket resting in the shallow water.

"Coffee?" Kathy asked.

"Acorn coffee," I said. "Rachel is doing research with acorns."

"Oh, yes. So I've heard."

We stood there in silence. Henry had been a good host to visitors at Walden Pond, but what about visitors who thought he was a lunatic?

"If you'd like, I could show you around," I suggested to Kathy. I remembered the tour guides at Greystone Colonial Village who lead people through the historic buildings; maybe I could act like they do and calmly take them on a tour of the Old Grove and then Hollis's feeding stations. Then I could show them the shortcut that would lead them back to Middleton before Rachel returned with her gunnysack. I gestured awkwardly toward the slope.

"Let me show you the lake," I said, as if anyone needed it pointed out. Stuart and Kathy followed me to the bluff above the water, but unfortunately we arrived just in time to see Rachel below us, dragging a waterlogged bushel basket onto the shore with a rope. Rachel had underestimated the weight of the soaking acorns, and with the effort of every pull she fell backward onto the sand in a sitting position.

"We have a canoe now, and take it all over the lake," I said, hoping to distract them.

"What's she doing?" Kathy said.

"She keeps the acorns out there. If you'll step this way, I'll show you the Old Grove."

"She keeps them in the water?" Kathy asked, curling up her nose.

"Well, yes, the water takes the bitterness out. Why don't you walk over here—there's a beautiful spot." I led them back into the trees.

"And we call this the Old Grove because it's the ancient part of the forest." I put my hand on a stump, trying to look like the proper tour guide stroking an antique armoire.

"How old is it?" Kathy wondered.

"Oh, hundreds of years, at least," I told her.

"Gosh," she sighed, and looked up at Stuart.

"And this huge trunk we call the submarine tree, for obvious reasons. Up in that hollow, way up there . . . a great horned owl is roosting. And right about here, Stuart created his fabulous map." I hadn't meant to say that. It just came out. Kathy studied the patch of ground respectfully.

I kept the tour brief, skipping the wild herbs and bird stations since Kathy was having trouble picking her way down even the easy paths. I wound them back to the cabin, hoping to reach the trailhead before Rachel and her slimy acorns, but she was already inside the cabin, spooning black acorn mush into a kettle. Before I could find a way to stop them, they had gone inside the cabin too.

"How cute!" Kathy cried.

"You put in a window," Stuart said. "And the walls are filled in."

They hadn't yet seen Hollis, who was sitting cross-legged in a corner, his sketchbook in his lap, coloring the rust-and-gray-striped tail of his ruffed grouse. Kathy tripped over him when she tried to look more closely at his bird chart.

"I'm so sorry!" She used his shoulder to steady herself. Hollis got up apologetically and stood half bowing and bobbing in the green light of the window.

"That's all right. I'm okay," he said. He was unnerved to see Kathy's pretty form so close, her soft, fair hair haloed by the doorway. She drew up next to him to see his sketch.

"Did you draw this?" she asked, and took the sketch pad from him.

"Yeah." He shrugged. "It's not very good, though." He scratched his head. "See? The neck is too fat."

"Oh, Stu, look at this! He's very talented." Stuart joined Kathy and together they flipped through the pages of "The Ones Who Stayed Behind" as Hollis shyly accepted their compliments.

Rachel sat by the stove, like an intent little witch, stirring the simmering acorn meal. She silently mimicked Kathy for me: *Oh, Stu!*

Stop it! I mouthed back.

Hollis sat spellbound while Kathy pored over his sketchbook, making little exclamations at every drawing and oohing over the feathers he'd found and taped to the pages. Stuart had turned his attention to *The World of Walden*, spread out on the table. He was reading passages and sometimes smiling to himself.

"Don't lose our place," Rachel told him sternly as she strained the acorn mixture through a sieve. "Watch out for the bookmark."

"I'll be careful," he said.

"Well, here it is," Rachel finally declared. "Wilderness coffee."

Kathy gave Stuart a frightened look, as if she were about to be initiated into some tribal ritual, but he ignored her and accepted the steaming cup Rachel handed him. Kathy took hers with an uncertain thank-you.

"Maybe they'd like some sugar in it," I said. "Don't we have some sugar?"

Kathy looked up hopefully, but Rachel was determined they should drink it "naturally." Hollis and I knew well that acorn coffee was barely palatable without generous amounts of milk and sugar.

"No, they won't need sugar. I've had this batch buried in the sand for almost three weeks. The longer they sit in there, the more tannic acid is leached out." Rachel squatted down on the floor and pulled the soggy gunnysack out from under her chair. She scooped a handful of the acorn meal and held it out to Kathy.

"See how rich and black that is? The blacker it gets, the

sweeter it is. Smell it," she said. Kathy gave Stuart another helpless look but took a tiny sniff.

"No, no. You've got to get your nose right down in there for the full aroma. Try again." Rachel held the acorn meal so close to Kathy's nose, I think she inhaled some. "Has a sort of nutty smell, doesn't it?" Rachel said.

"So does the coffee," Stuart said, sipping his thoughtfully. Rachel took a gulp from her own cup and sighed with satisfaction.

Kathy inched her cup down and set it on the floor. "I wouldn't do that," Rachel said, shaking her head. "All kinds of critters run around in here, wood rats, mice, moles. They're crazy about acorn coffee and will sip it right out of your cup when you're not looking. They'll even run up your leg if they think you've got food."

Horrified, Kathy grabbed up her coffee and raised her feet off the floor. Hollis and I traded looks and tried not to smile.

"If you leave the acorns in water long enough, they'll get moldy; let's see if I've got any forming in here." Rachel dug around in the damp bag. "Ah yes, here's a lovely sample." She reached out and smeared the moldy paste across Kathy's hand.

Kathy shrieked and looked for some way to wipe it off. "Oh, don't worry—it's good for you! Some Indian tribes," Rachel continued, "used to scrape off the mold and then rub it into sores. It was an antibiotic! Who would think that something so delicious could also cure an oozing infection!"

"Yes, who would think," Kathy said angrily. She stood up. "I'm afraid I have to be going now. Stu?"

Without waiting for him, without saying good-bye to Hollis, without even tasting her wilderness coffee, Kathy left the cabin and probably all of Wayburn Woods for good. Stuart had no choice but to leave with her, although I think he would rather have stayed with us and finished his coffee, even without milk and sugar.

I walked them as far as the Old Grove. Kathy walked on ahead of us, climbing the path with surprising vigor. Perhaps Rachel was right about the virtues of wilderness coffee: it seemed the aroma alone had filled Kathy Dulack with new vitality. Stuart lingered a bit with his hands in his pockets.

"We didn't get a chance to discuss our presentation for Friday. But I was thinking that Hollis should go first, then Rachel, then you. I'll finish up by showing the map. That way we'll end by giving them the big picture."

"That sounds fine," I said.

"When we first came today . . . I didn't mean to say that you were strange, Beth. I think it's great that you've kept up the experiment. Henry David Thoreau would be proud of you." He sounded like himself again, before he became a corporate executive, and for an instant I almost poured out everything that had happened in the forest since he had stopped coming.

"You should come by more often, Stuart."

"Thanks," he said, smiling. "I'll try. I really will." But I felt as if we were standing on opposite sides of a rushing stream that was becoming so loud I could barely hear him. He started up the path back to Middleton Road, and I watched him until he disappeared in the alder trees.

Chapter 10

"Public opinion is a weak tyrant compared with our own private opinion. What a man thinks of himself, that is which determines, or rather indicates, his fate."
H. D. THOREAU

Kathy Dulack had never been friendly to me, but when I saw her in homeroom the next day, she was downright aloof. I shuddered to think what she had told her friends about her visit to the cabin.

"You didn't have to push that acorn coffee on them," I told Rachel as we climbed the stairs to Mrs. Stark's classroom. "It was bad enough to have them there—why did you encourage them to stay? You practically forced that concoction down their throats!"

"Trust me, not a drop touched Kathy's lips, and if it had, it would have done her a world of good." I couldn't make

Rachel feel guilty about their visit. She believed acorns were the soul of the forest, "our medicine," and if they could keep snooty girls from nosing around the cabin, so much the better.

In Mrs. Stark's room the lights were dimmed and the desks had been arranged into theater seating around a large-screen television.

"What's all this?" I whispered to Rachel as we entered.

She squinted at the "We Went to the Woods" board. "Must be the Larry, Chip, and Ben Show. They're the only group scheduled for today."

The class sat in an awed stillness while Chip efficiently clicked the audiovisual equipment into readiness. The television screen lit up cobalt blue with their title frame: WILDER-NESS WEEKEND. The three of them held a last-minute huddle off to the side and ended it with a spirited high five. Larry swaggered to the podium.

"When we thought about doing this *Walden* project, my very first thought . . . was that the best place to do it would be . . . my uncle's cabin in Otsabo!" The class burst into wild clapping.

"It's a good thing the ski season hadn't started, or I don't know if we could've resisted hitting the slopes, if you know what I mean." Larry looked out at the class as if the term *hitting the slopes* disguised some kind of secret message for all the skiers in the audience. Again, the room erupted in applause.

"Anyway, my uncle said okay, and so that's where we went." Larry pointed a finger at the television.

That was Chip's signal to begin the movie. We were treated to twenty minutes of the boys' hilarious visit to Uncle Brad's A-frame cabin in the Otsabo Mountain Resort. The film was a technological wonder; they'd used fade-ins, fade-outs, and even slow-motion sequences. It began with a close-up of each boy as he stepped out of Mrs. Duncan's van and stared pensively at the lovely fall colors on the wooded hills. But it quickly dissolved into goofy group scenes with unnecessary subtitles for each segment: "Building a Campfire," "Marking the Trail," "Using a First Aid Kit." Every scene started with Larry demonstrating a simplistic survival skill and ended with all of them clowning around and waving at the camera. There were even outtakes so we could see the fun they'd had making mistakes. It was witless, shallow, insincere, and—as far as the class was concerned—absolutely dazzling.

The final image of Larry, Chip, and Ben hadn't yet faded from the screen, and the *Star Wars* theme song was still washing over us, when the class rose to its feet. This was the show they'd been waiting for. As Mrs. Stark tried to quiet the applause and get the class back into chairs, everyone knew that Presentation Week was essentially over. Where could we go from there? We'd reached the pinnacle of excellence.

At the cabin that afternoon we didn't discuss the movie; we just finished up our projects with quiet anxiety. For weeks Rachel had been boiling acorns over and over, pouring the acidic water into the sand. When the nuts were sweet enough, she had roasted them in a skillet and used rocks to grind them into meal. A mound of this brown mash had been forming on the table, but up until then she'd been tight-lipped about Presentation Day.

"All I can tell you is that I'm going to demonstrate some techniques with acorns. Believe me, the final product will be a showstopper."

I wondered how acorns could compete with the breathtaking sight of Larry Duncan leaping over a stream in slow motion. But if Rachel believed her acorns could top that, I wouldn't doubt her. She had become something of a miracle herself. In six weeks she had changed from a girl into a frontier woman, struggling up the slope with water buckets, fueling her stove with sticks, pounding rock against rock until her fingers bled. She mixed the acorn meal with flour and water and kneaded it with such vigor that she could speak only in fragments.

"Builds the gluten. No leavening. Thoreau didn't use yeast. Not necessary. Just mold it, bake it." She opened the belly of the stove and her face glowed in its heat.

"It's too hot. I need rocks or the bottom will scorch." We stacked stones as evenly as we could on the stovetop and she placed the bread in an iron pan with a lid. Rachel's grand finale had only two hours to bake.

We were all racing sunset. Hollis hadn't lifted his head from the slope all afternoon. He was still gathering insect remains.

"I can finish up the model at home tonight," he said anxiously. "But I need more bodies, more evidence."

"Hollis," I said carefully, "why don't you show your bird sketches tomorrow instead of the bugs? You could tell them about 'The Ones Who Stayed Behind.' You could show them your chart—your chart is wonderful."

Hollis wasn't used to compliments. He smiled and looked away. "You really think I should?"

"Yes, I think you should show the birds."

He thought for a few moments, probably skimming through his sketchbook in his mind. "Nope, I'll stick with the bugs," he said suddenly. "The bugs for sure."

I understood his choice, though I knew it wasn't the better one. I had carefully selected the pages from my journal that I would read for Presentation Day, and they weren't the best ones, but they were the safest ones.

I was the last to leave that afternoon. Rachel trudged solemnly back to the Haygen house with her buckets, and Hollis mounted his bike with the insect coffin balanced on his open palm. I'm sure Stuart was somewhere tapping his fingers on his rolled map, eager to show it to the world tomorrow, but I was sick with dread.

Mrs. Stark must have known that *Wilderness Weekend* was going to be a tough act to follow, because on Friday afternoon she gave us a rousing introduction. "I must say, class, it is with deep regret that we bring Presentation Week to a close. However, to use an old adage, we've saved the best for last! Rachel, Beth, Hollis, Stuart, please come forward. We're all looking forward to what I am certain will be an insightful and inspiring conclusion."

Rising numbly, I saw peripherally that Hollis, Rachel,

and Stuart were gathering their bundles and heading to the front.

Hollis wrote *Insect Warfare* on the board. Then he took a heavy breath and held out his bug box. "This is not what you think it is," he began. The class looked perplexed, having no inkling what it was.

"No, I'm not going to give a report on entomology because you've heard that before. Who hasn't had a collection of bugs and pinned them onto cardboard and labeled all their parts?" He laughed nervously, but Mrs. Stark's class had been hardened by four days of nature talk and they watched him laugh in cold silence.

"So I'm not going to bore you with that approach. Instead, I like to think of myself as an insect detective, because I've tried to solve the mysteries surrounding the death of these bugs. How did they die? Where did it happen? Were they victims or were they the aggressors?"

I saw the beginnings of twisted smiles. Hollis continued with his bug theories, not realizing that the animation in everyone's eyes was ridicule, not interest. The hinges on his bug coffin were overly tight, so when he sprung open the lid a flurry of wings and skeletons puffed out and settled on Camilla Rodgers's desk. She squealed and brushed them violently onto the floor.

"That's all right," Hollis said. "I've got plenty more." He lifted the head of a grasshopper from the satin lining with tweezers and held it up.

"Here's a good example. Now, how did this guy lose his head? He might have died at the end of the summer like most grasshoppers, but maybe it's not that simple. Under magnification, I found that there are jagged edges at the base of his skull. So who did it? A raiding grasshopper? A jealous mate? These are the questions an insect detective tries to answer."

Just then the grasshopper head slipped, and Hollis, who was amazingly quick with those tweezers, grasped it in midair as it tumbled toward Camilla. She screamed and cowered behind her notebook. Whatever scientific credibility Hollis had established up to then ended when the class heard the crunch of the head as it broke in the pinch of tweezers and fell like a shattered cornflake over Camilla's clean hair.

Mrs. Stark let the laughter rage for a few moments, and then she warned us with one fierce clap of her hands. The class quieted and settled back, hoping more accidents over Camilla's head would be forthcoming.

I saw Stuart give Hollis a reassuring nod as he picked up his posterboard. Hollis held up his Wanted poster, a collage of insect pieces glued to the cardboard. "Now, these are the bugs that may be responsible for decapitating the grasshopper. These are the suspects, you might say. You may be wondering why they look so large and colorful." *Distorted* and *deformed* were better words to describe the creatures that Hollis had drawn from the existing body parts.

"I drew the whole insect as it probably appeared to the grasshopper just before he . . . lost his head."

I thought at the time, as the class howled with laughter, that the old movie channel on cable television had not been good for Hollis. He'd seen too many King Kongs, too many crab monsters, and too many giant moths. I should have insisted that he bring his bird sketches. They were simple and real and no one would have laughed.

He still had one more item to display, the cigar box. On the bottom he had glued a few real carcasses, and then he had drawn in troops of ladybugs, june beetles, and cicadas. Some even carried little spears. I didn't think the class could take it. A few were close to hysteria.

Mrs. Stark finally intervened, not to rescue Hollis as I hoped, but to face him with a final indignity. "Hollis, I don't believe you've mentioned Mr. Thoreau yet, and I'm not quite clear how this relates to him. Could you explain the connection for us?"

Hollis was stunned. Of course he hadn't mentioned Henry. Digging bugs out of the slope and caring about their lives had everything to do with Henry. But he stood frozen and voiceless over the coffin and the cardboard battlefield, unable to defend himself.

Stuart wasn't about to let Hollis squirm indefinitely, though, nor was he going to let our presentation fizzle out so soon. He stepped forward. "Mrs. Stark, Hollis is referring to the chapter called 'Brute Neighbors' in *Walden,* where Henry David Thoreau describes the battling ants that he had found locked in combat. He took three home, two red ones pitted against a black one, and put them on his windowsill to observe their fight." Stuart was searching his copy of *Walden*. "If you'll give us a second, I could find the page."

"No, that isn't necessary." Mrs. Stark waved off the page number. "I didn't realize your group had used the unabridged *Walden*. How impressive! And what a creative way to explore Mr. Thoreau's keen observation of even the smallest creatures. Thank you, Hollis. Who is next? Go right ahead, Rachel."

Rachel turned to the chalkboard and wrote *Cuisine of the Forest* in large, graceful cursive. She had spread her cooking demonstration across three of the front desks. We waited while she checked and arranged her ingredients, bowls, spoons, bucket, and a secret lump wrapped in wax paper on Mrs. Stark's desk. She flicked her stringy hair back, pushed her glasses into place, and began.

"I'm going to make acorn bread to show that there are many sources of food in the forest that you wouldn't expect. Things that you just walk over all the time can actually be nutritious and pretty tasty."

If Rachel had been more relaxed, she might have pulled off this unusual demonstration, but her nervousness showed from the start when she held out the bowl of soaking acorns and the water sloshed in her trembling hands. If she had been an attractive, popular girl, the class might have enjoyed her cooking show. But since it was just homely Rachel explaining the importance of soaking the ground acorn meal to leach out the bitterness, no one was interested. When she held out the thick paste, the masa, that would be formed into patties and baked on hot rocks, obviously, this was a food experience too exotic for most kids. They stifled their giggles and made mock gagging sounds.

Mrs. Stark loved Rachel. What teacher wouldn't? She turned in her neat and thorough work on time. She could be counted on to answer any question, at any time, though her attention was usually diverted to a novel. She was the kind of student who made teachers look good, because even if the instruction was bungling and dull, Rachel's incisive mind quickly grasped the essential points, and she taught herself. So Mrs. Stark prowled the aisles protectively while the bread lesson droned on, hoping to catch one of the retching listeners.

Rachel was betrayed by her nerves but not her courage. She didn't skip a single detail she thought important. "For variety, you can add buckwheat flowers, and that will give the bread a crunchy texture. Also, pollen from cattail spikes can be rubbed into the dough to make it a golden color."

She had stopped looking at the class as a whole and was addressing Marjorie Winfred and Janice Phelson, the only students who were still listening politely. Her voice was steady, but she gleamed with perspiration, and seemingly her glasses were sliding down her nose so fast that only constant pressure from her knuckle would hold them up.

A hundred things went wrong: when she flung the ground acorns into the air to show how the husks would fly off in the breeze, a huge wave of acorn meal simply crashed on the floor, husks and all. The masa clung to her fingers so tenaciously that she had to twist it off with a towel, until her fingers looked swollen and red. Then, when she felt she had warned us of every possible pitfall in making acorn bread, she revealed the finished loaf from under its cover.

She held it out humbly, as if she more than anyone were awed by its existence. If ever there was a noble and fitting monument to Henry, it had to be that rough nut-brown oval resting in Rachel's chapped hands. Nothing we had seen that week was its equal in purity and hard-won toughness.

Being such a hearty bread, though, it didn't cut easily. Rachel had to balance her whole body over the knife in order to cut little pieces for the class to sample.

"Rachel, dear." Mrs. Stark took the tray of samples from her. "Why don't we let the students take their samples as they leave. Then they won't feel rushed." I'll bet Larry and Chip were especially eager to get their hands on those bread cubes, though savoring the texture was not what they had in mind. Mrs. Stark led the class in halfhearted applause for Rachel's "remarkably detailed and well-researched presentation." And then it was my turn.

They must have wondered who I was when I materialized at the front of the room, an invisible girl who had never spoken in class. Without any explanation I opened my journal to the first entry, the one I'd written late at night when the cabin was new. As I read, something curious happened. My words, like a powerful current, pulled them along with me. I led them down the paths of Wayburn Woods, seated them in the Old Grove, and showed them how the cabin had taken shape under the towering trees. I closed my notebook and sensed they were sorry I'd stopped.

Stuart stepped up and I helped him unroll his map. He had charred the edges of it with a wood-burning tool, making it look like an ancient treasure map. Kids in the back three rows stood up from their seats to get a better look. Janice caught her breath. Larry's mouth went slack. "This is totally amazing," he said.

Compliments came from everywhere.

"Great job, Stuart!"

"Way to go, Garfield!"

"Speech! Speech!" Ben called.

Stuart grinned and was gradually persuaded to explain how he had so brilliantly drawn the area to scale. He elaborated on the many challenges he had faced while "surveying" the Old Grove. I watched the spectacle, fascinated. Hands were shooting up. The class was suddenly interested in the names of trees, in mapping techniques. And was it just me, or was Stuart starting to sound like those stuffy narrators on safari expeditions?

The truth is, they had no idea how remarkable that map was. You had to know Wayburn like I did to appreciate the wonder of it. No, it was Stuart they were gushing over, not his map. Just as Rachel had predicted, he had gone beyond being popular: he had become their leader.

Stuart raised his hand for silence. "Thanks, you guys. But this map is just a piece of paper. Even our Henry Contract"—he looked over at us—"was just a piece of paper.

Our experiment was a success because my partners were dedicated and worked hard. And I want to thank them for that." Stuart, the politician, led the class in a round of applause for us. I stared down at the floor, my face flushed from the attention. Rachel would be fuming!

"Even the *Pine Press* is just a pile of papers," Stuart continued. "It's what all of *you* contribute—the stories, the ideas—that's what makes it special, that's what makes it a success."

The class was so moved, they didn't applaud. Mrs. Stark clutched her hands, speechless. I couldn't wait to sit down, to slip back into invisibility, to be swallowed up by the passing period. But Stuart just wouldn't quit.

"By the way, you'll all be hearing more about Wayburn Woods very soon," he said, glancing our way again. "Don't miss the next issue of the *Press!*"

What did he mean by that? Our bowed heads snapped up. You couldn't find more opposite expressions than were on the faces of my group—Rachel, glaring at Stuart, her suspicions standing on end like porcupine quills; and Stuart, smiling proudly as he rolled up his map.

Chapter 11

"I have a great deal of company in my house;
especially in the morning, when nobody calls."
H. D. Thoreau

As promised, Wayburn Woods was front-page news the next week. This special holiday issue was passed out on Monday. Stuart, as editor in chief, had created a new, permanent column entitled "Notes from the Woods," by Beth Gardner. My first article, "The Rescue of Gort," all four hundred words of it, had been printed under the title.

Rachel was outraged. "How could he *print* that?" she asked.

"Well, you're the one who tried to poison his girl-friend," I said.

"Wait a minute. He can't get away with this. There are laws about publishing without the author's permission. He must have taken your journal when he was here and had that secretary of his copy it. We'll sue him for this. We'll sue the *Press* for every dime it's ever made!"

"No, we won't sue, because he didn't steal it, Rachel. I turned this in to Mrs. Stark; it was an assignment."

"What assignment?"

"I don't remember," I lied. "Just some descriptive assignment."

"Well, it's descriptive, all right. You've described us like complete morons." She reread the column as we sat in the clearing outside the cabin, and it made her furious all over again.

"We'll sue Mrs. Stark too—she can't go selling student work. She's probably in cahoots with him; they all are! Just because of that ridiculous newspaper!"

"It's nobody's fault, Rachel. I turned it in as a feature article. I never thought he'd print it. Mrs. Stark said to write about important events, so I wrote about . . . an important event. But it didn't seem like something the *Press* would consider important. I guess you'll just have to sue me."

She went inside and made some hot chocolate and left it warming in a pan until Hollis arrived. I understood her frustration. It was disconcerting to imagine the whole school reading about us, reliving that morning when we fed the geese and saved Gort. How much more visible could we get?

Hollis trotted up to the cabin with the *Press* tucked underneath his arm.

"Have you seen it?" he asked.

"Yes," I said. "I'm sorry, Hollis."

"Why? I think it's neat. We're on the cover." He snapped the paper open to look at it again. Rachel gave him some cocoa.

"Will you think it's so 'neat' when kids start calling you goose-catcher or Gort-face?" Hollis gave this some thought but was still unconcerned.

"Henry was probably made fun of," I ventured to say. "I'll bet people in Concord considered him a real weirdo."

"Yes, but Henry didn't have to go to school," Rachel said. She examined the *Press* over Hollis's shoulder. "How many of these descriptions have you turned in to Mrs. Stark, anyway?" she asked.

"Lots," I said.

"You'd better talk to Stuart."

We had record-breaking cold weather in the few days before Thanksgiving—no snow, but freezing temperatures that turned the inlet into a mirror of thin ice and forced all of us into heavy coats and gloves. Mother drove me to school on Tuesday, so that I could beat the crowds from the buses and catch Stuart in the *Press* office before first period.

I opened the door and found Kathy at her desk, writing what looked to be a note to a friend.

"Yes?" she asked.

"Is Stuart here? I'd like to talk to him," I said.

"He's interviewing Mr. Owens and the honor roll students," she said, and went back to her correspondence.

"Will he be in here during lunch?"

She exhaled loudly and put her pen down.

"Lunch? Today? Let's see." She searched through an appointment calendar. "No, he's going off campus with Mr. Erikson. They're going to see about some sponsors for the paper."

"What about after school?" I asked.

"I'm afraid not. He has plans." She smiled slightly, telling me she was part of those plans.

I stopped by his office on Wednesday, and Stuart was on the phone with more potential sponsors. The *Press* was about to enter its "new phase." Stuart was trying to get local businesses to advertise in the *Press*. His promotional speech over the PA system that morning encouraged us to do our part.

"Help the *Press* expand its size and its reach! Commercial advertising will bring more recognition for PBS in our community and more money for a better paper!" Some scattered cheering was heard from various homerooms when Stuart added that *sponsor prizes* would be awarded to students who could drum up the most business.

"Naturally," Rachel said to me at lunch. "The *Press* is not a newspaper; it's a game show. What worries me, though, is this idea of expanding the audience and selling the paper at local businesses, the mall . . . Blitz's! Find him, Beth. Stop him before we get exposed all over the state!"

I walked into the *Press* office that afternoon, determined to outwit Kathy Dulack and her appointment book. Both she and Cindy Wedford were collating and stapling papers.

"Do you have an appointment?" Kathy asked.

"No, but I need to talk to Stuart," I said. Cindy walked up to the desk, implying that she would handle this.

"Well, he's not available."

"This is urgent. When will he be here?" I asked.

"I have no idea. . . . Perhaps you'd like to leave a message?" she said, handing me a notepad and pencil.

I was tempted until I realized that Cindy and Kathy would read the message first and Stuart might never see it. I needed a new approach. I sat down on the edge of the visitor's chair.

"I might as well tell you, I suppose. I'm just so eager to find out which of my articles he's printing next week. We had discussed several, but I'm dying to find out if he picked 'An Owl of Our Own' or 'Cabin Fever.' But I guess your job is mostly stapling and you wouldn't know that sort of thing."

"I know what's going on around here," Kathy said. "I can tell you exactly what article we've printed, because the new issue is already done." Triumphantly, she held out a newly stapled copy to me, but Cindy grabbed it back as I reached for it.

"You'll have to wait, like everyone else," she said. "But I can tell you, it was neither of those. It's called 'The Buffalo Berry Hunt.'"

"Oh good!" I rose and gathered my books. "We were hoping he'd choose that one, especially Rachel. You know how she likes to talk about wild plants!"

"Yes, I know," Kathy said.

I decided not to tell Rachel about the upcoming article; it would only increase her paranoia.

The new and improved *Pine Press* was issued to students free in homeroom the week after Thanksgiving, and it went onto the shelves of a dozen businesses around town for fifty cents a copy. "We're a real newspaper now," Stuart announced over the PA system. "Pine Brook School now has a bridge to the world!"

I don't think many students shared Stuart's vision for the *Press*. Most kids skimmed the feature articles to see who would get prizes, and then scanned "Sports Spots" for the names of friends. They might stop at "Pressing Problems," the student advice column, or they might try "Press This," the math brain teaser of the week. Sure, the advertisements were tantalizing because they offered free dance tickets and buy-one-get-one-free burgers at Blitz's, but only Stuart saw the sponsor page as "our bridge to the world."

Just as I feared, the printing of "The Buffalo Berry Hunt" mortified Rachel.

"I thought you were going to have this stopped," she said.

"I couldn't. He's hard to reach. But I promise I'll try next week. This one will be the last."

On Saturday we cleaned the cabin and restocked our firewood. Then together we hiked all day along the lake into unexplored groves and meadows. As long as we kept moving, the chill of early December couldn't get its teeth into us. And we heard new sounds in Wayburn: the sharp whistle of wind, the shatter of frostbitten grass, the stir of preparation, and at times, the enormous silence that heralded snow.

Chapter 12

"Follow your genius closely enough, and it will not fail to
show you a fresh prospect every hour."
H. D. THOREAU

Rachel had worried for nothing. None of the terrible things
she had imagined came true. Nobody teased her; nobody
even mentioned buffalo berries. The worst comment was the
one Brendan Fain made to her at lunch one day. As he
tromped by with his tray, he slowed and eyed the beige gravy
over his slice of meat loaf.

"Say, Rachel, you ought to take these cooks out to the
woods with you and teach them a few tricks." It was the most
daring statement Brendan had ever made, and he looked back
to the lunch line to be sure the stern-faced ladies behind the
counter hadn't heard him. Rachel blushed while Brendan
stood by us, laughing quietly as the gravy jiggled on his plate.

"I think he likes you, Rachel," I said after he'd gone. She blushed again and pushed her glasses up.

"I mean it. I've sat behind Brendan all year in sixth period, and we've come to understand each other."

"Oh, be quiet," she said.

By the time our third article was in print, Rachel was attracting all sorts of friendly attention. I was behind her in the hall one morning and heard at least three unknown voices greet her, kind voices calling out things like "Hey Rachel! How are those acorns doing?" Luckily I witnessed it for myself, for she would have never told me. Just as I would never have known about Ralph Donnely, our star center on the basketball team, approaching her before homeroom had I not seen him myself. He pulled a plastic bag of acorns from his book bag.

"I thought you might like these," he said. "They're from the oak tree my mom planted. She's nuts about that tree." He laughed at himself. "Get it? Nuts about nuts, kind of like you. Anyway, maybe you can use them for your experiment. See ya, Rachel!" He bounced away while Rachel clutched the bag and started breathing again.

But the most enthusiastic attention Rachel received was from the Rare and Indigenous Plant Society of Michigan. Ms. Adela Thomas, president of the Meadowcreek Hills chapter, had happened on a copy of the *Press* at her hairdresser's. In a letter to Rachel she said she was "simply astounded to read about such an accomplished young botanist." It seems Rachel had sighted a rare form of blue gentian, a late-blooming wildflower. Members of the society had been scouring the Michigan countryside unsuccessfully for years, and here Rachel had stumbled onto the gentian while looking for plain old buffalo berries.

The plant had shriveled under the frost, so a positive identification couldn't be made, but the ladies took Rachel's word for it. They planned to make a pilgrimage to the spot next fall to see the miracle for themselves. Rachel had no idea that she had made such a rare find, but the ladies of the flower society knew they'd made a rare find in Rachel. They invited her to a meeting of the chapter and made her an honorary member of the society. They even gave her a medal! Her picture appeared in the *Detroit News*, and over thirty students submitted essays on "Rachel's discovery" for their feature article that week.

Not long after the hubbub over Rachel calmed down, Hollis showed up at the cabin one afternoon without his sketch pad, his arms looking strangely empty.

"What's wrong?" Rachel asked.

"Nothing," he said.

"You look different. Your sketchbook. Where is it?"

I could see why she was alarmed. Hollis carried his sketchbook everywhere. He had to. His search for birds was constant and unpredictable. They didn't have to be unusual; he was as eager to sketch a blue jay perched on a fence as he was a downy woodpecker deep in Wayburn Woods. The book's cover was sun-bleached, stained, sticky with sap, its corners curled up. Sometimes it was stashed between math and American history books, or between damp moss and dry leaves. It could fly too, like the birds on its pages, into the cabin in heavy rains, onto the bottom of the green canoe, but it was never, ever left behind.

"Where is it, Hollis?" asked Rachel, rising.

"Mr. Mitchell took it," he said.

Rachel and I looked at each other and had the same thought. The class had probably been rotating through lab stations and Hollis, unaware, had stayed at his desk, shading the feathers of some bird.

"You got in trouble?" I asked.

"No, Mr. Mitchell asked me if he could take it. He liked it, I guess. He wants to take pictures of my drawings."

Mr. Mitchell developed them in his own basement dark-room, and when they were done, Hollis previewed them after school in the empty science lab. The slide projector hummed and Mr. Mitchell flashed one bird after another onto the screen.

"They were mega-birds!" Hollis told us. "A three-inch black-capped chickadee was the size of a German shepherd! And oh man, every pencil line was thick and wide like I'd used a paintbrush."

He also saw his mistakes: awkward legs, oversize heads, cartoonish eyes. Yet overall, maybe Hollis saw what Mr. Mitchell must have seen. Slowly, with every erasure and with every bird he sketched and then sketched again, Hollis was becoming an artist.

"Mr. Mitchell wants to use the pictures for a lecture he's

doing. He wants me to help him narrate it, so kids can learn about nonmigratory Michigan birds."

"Are you sure that's a good idea?" Rachel asked. She remembered Hollis's bug presentation with the same anguish that I did.

"You didn't want to show your pictures before, remember?" I said.

"Yeah, but it's different now," he assured us. "I've improved."

During the week before Christmas vacation, Hollis was excused from his other subjects and became a guest speaker in Mr. Mitchell's science classes. Hollis worked the remote control, lighting up darkened classrooms with American goldfinches and northern cardinals. He used a yardstick to point out the birds' unique features, and told stories about them as if they were pets. He imitated their songs and no one laughed except Hollis, because sometimes he surprised himself with his own accuracy.

As the author of "Notes from the Woods," I was dutifully cranking out my weekly articles, but I wasn't getting any special attention at school other than my tiny byline in the *Press*. I didn't even get a prize for being a feature journalist. My only passionate fans were Mr. McDuff and my mother. Mr. McDuff took out a full-page ad in the *Press* for McDuff Realty and bought me a laptop computer.

On the Friday before Christmas break, the first snow flurries came sifting down like confetti. Rachel and I watched their slow dance from the windows of the bus and savored the two weeks of freedom that stretched ahead.

We dumped our books at the Haygen house and started down the path. Every tree and turn in the trail looked unfamiliar, veiled under a thin film of snow. We had tea when Hollis arrived and discussed our Christmas plans.

"My cousins from Detroit are coming out," Rachel told us. "All seven of them. So I won't be able to come out here for a few days."

"Me neither. We're having company too," I said. Mother was preparing a food extravaganza for Mr. McDuff and me. I'd heard about the cornbread-oyster dressing and pecan pie all week as I helped her polish the sterling. Only Hollis didn't seem to have any obligations he could grumble about. Even on Christmas he was as footloose as he always was, and as disinclined to talk about his family.

Rachel knew very little about Hollis, considering they lived only a half mile apart. His mother looked very young and thin and drove all the way to Baymont Hospital every night, where she worked as a nurse in the emergency room. That explained why Hollis never had to hurry home after our makeshift meals in the cabin. He often volunteered to stay and stir down the fire or clean up the dishes while Rachel and I grabbed flashlights and ran home along the path. Hollis had an older brother, Phil, who worked in a hardware store or maybe at the Drexter plant. Rachel didn't think they had a father.

On Christmas Eve day we all managed to meet at the cabin for a few hours, and we tied some pine boughs over the window. Rachel arranged red candles on the card table and Hollis hung some tinsel on Gort's Trophy, but we had our official Christmas on the twenty-eighth, after Rachel's cousins had gone and the household was down to a mere fifteen again.

I couldn't tell if Rachel liked her gift. She looked over the small leather purse doubtfully.

"Thanks, Beth, it's really nice." I don't think she knew what to put inside it. Rachel didn't even carry a comb.

The best part was giving Hollis his gifts, mainly because we suspected he hadn't received many at home. Rachel and I had pooled our money and bought him some expensive colored pencils and a book about the life of John James Audubon.

"He was one of the first wildlife artists," Rachel explained. "He's famous for his life-size bird portraits."

Hollis looked through the pictures. He seemed amazed that someone else had thought of drawing birds too, particularly life-size ones.

I wanted to stay later that day, like Hollis and Rachel did, to lounge around the cabin while the candles still burned and work in my journal, but I promised my mother I'd be home before dark. She and Mr. McDuff were going house scouting, something they did frequently, and insisted that I join them. The evening lay ahead of me like miles of boring terrain. We would give two or three homes in Meadowcreek Hills the McDuff Realty walk-through and then go to a movie. The best part, according to my mother, was that I could wear some of my new clothes.

Almost every box under the tree had been for me. Mother had spent most of her recent bonuses on giving me "the kind of Christmas we used to have." I lifted layers of tissue paper to find new boots, sweaters, jeans. Even the queen of them all, a Glamma Girl outfit, fell into my lap that Christmas morning. After Mr. McDuff found out how important Glamma Girl clothes were, he bought me an outfit that would turn even Kathy Dulack's head. I had to unwrap three boxes before the entire collection was revealed: a flowered skirt, a matching cashmere sweater set, pants, jacket, and shoes with a bright red *G* sewn into the back of the heel.

"Oh, I don't know, Louis," my mother fretted, holding the sweater up to me, "maybe we should have gone with the heather blue instead of the sage green."

"She'll look lovely in either," he said. "Go back and buy the heather too, so there'll be no doubt."

"Heavens no!" she said. "Beth, what do you think?"

"The sage is fine," I said, fingering the delicate wool. It was strange to hold something so powerful. You couldn't be invisible in Glamma Girl clothes. How could such a flimsy piece of fabric do so much? No wonder Henry warned us about clothes. He said, "Beware of all enterprises that require new clothes, and not rather a new wearer of clothes." What would he think of my new outfit?

I thought about this as I walked home, away from the forest and back to the neat and organized neighborhoods off

Middleton. I could smell the smoke from fireplaces, and maybe our smoke in Wayburn was mixed in as well. At least the Glamma Girl outfit was green. I decided it was moss green, fern green, Old Grove green, and that I would wear it for an entirely different reason than everybody else did.

Chapter 13

"The squirrels also grew at last to be quite
familiar, and occasionally stepped upon
my shoe, when that was the nearest way."
H. D. THOREAU

By the time the real snows came, we were back in school, safely strapped into the monotony of Mrs. Stark's English class. We didn't get to see the white drifts mound in the corners of Wayburn Woods; instead, we read *Lord of the Flies* and watched the snow pile up next to the chain-link fence around the football field.

Mrs. Stark put up a bulletin board with big paper palm trees to represent the Pacific island in the novel where the boys are marooned. Marjorie donated a huge conch shell she'd bought in Miami, and Mrs. Stark passed it around for us to handle.

"From now on, no one may speak unless he or she is in

possession of the shell," she said. "In this way we can experience the struggle for leadership and order that is so central to this story."

For some reason Mrs. Stark expected us to shout and fight for that conch and scramble onto our desks to give speeches. We had never acted that way before. No one had much to say in January. Larry Duncan and Ben Jones were usually good for a few complaints, but they were conserving their energy for basketball practice. Stuart was a regular contributor, but he was rarely in class. He did his assignments independently and used class time for editing the *Pine Press*. So we were an extremely polite group of shipwrecked schoolchildren. We passed the conch shell back and forth and answered Mrs. Stark's comprehension questions. Poor Mrs. Stark just couldn't get us to care about the steamy island jungle. We were too heavy with gloves and hats and boots and the curtain of snow that never seemed to part.

Wayburn had become almost inaccessible. The northern drifts off Middleton Road were thigh-high, making the shortcut from the Haygen house a difficult hike. We worked after school for three days to pack down a trail with the Haygens' toboggan, but another four inches fell on Thursday and we had to give it up. No matter how we rushed after school, sundown was on our heels, and even when we reached the cabin, there wasn't time to kindle a fire before blue shadows fell and we had to hike out again.

But on Saturday the sun came out and we cleared paths

around the cabin with snow shovels, and then Hollis climbed into oak trees and shook down the remaining leaves. We scattered them on our paths to absorb the heat of the sun. Henry had told us about that and promised that our oak-lined trails would stay dry underfoot and guide us at night. We dug our firewood from a deep, powdery drift and fixed the tarp to keep it dry. Finally, we swept the snow from our doorway and moved into the cabin again.

Hollis worked frantically to empty his bird feeders of the mounds of snow they had accumulated. The garbage-can lids looked like gnome hats, and icicles clung to the edges like fringe. He worked all day, dragging bags of seed up the hill and along his network of feeding stations. Stephen helped him by pulling suet in a sled and tossing it up to him once Hollis was securely out on a tree limb.

"You should have seen the chickadees," Hollis said. "They've gotten so skinny. They watched me from the other trees, and I know they wonder why I'd stopped, why I hadn't come for so long." He shook his head in disgust. "I should've been out here sooner, snow or no snow."

"They're fine, Hollis. Birds always look thinner in winter," Rachel replied. But he was inconsolable. He didn't set foot in the cabin that day, even though Rachel made gingerbread in an iron skillet. He wandered home in the late afternoon, still muttering about his carelessness.

On Sunday morning the temperature rose to the low forties, and we threatened to shed our parkas if it got any warmer. Rachel spent the morning sorting through the pantry.

"We've got mice in the food crate," she announced. "Lots of them. They're probably living beneath these floorboards or wintering in the woodpile. I'll bring some traps out this week."

"Traps!" Hollis cried. "You can't use traps on them. You'll hurt them or even kill them!"

"That's the idea, Hollis. I can't have them scampering around our food; it's unhealthy. They've chewed right through the cornmeal bag; the maple candy is ruined. Look"— she tilted the crate—"their droppings are over everything."

"You can't do that here. You can't kill the animals; they were here first. I'm sure HDT never did that." He looked to me for help.

"I can't recall Henry killing any animals because they inconvenienced him," I said. "I remember that he fed the squirrels old ears of corn he'd saved. We read that part about the squirrels running around and performing like dancing girls."

"Yes! And he fed the rabbits potato parings in front of his door," Hollis added. "Remember *that*, Rachel!"

"Fine. Feed them all you want, but they're stealing our food and contaminating it," Rachel answered.

"Wait," he said. "Don't forget the woodchucks! They ate his beanfield, or at least part of it, remember? After he'd worked so hard to clear it and plant all those beans, and what was it he said?"

Hollis opened *Walden* and searched for "The Bean-Field." Rachel and I watched as Hollis, the reluctant reader, pored over the text like a lawyer hell-bent on finding a precedent.

"Here it is!" he shouted. "'My enemies are worms, cool days, and most of all woodchucks.' See? Woodchucks! Those are much worse than mice."

Rachel sighed. "Just read it."

"'The last have nibbled for me a quarter of an acre clean. But what right had I to oust johnswort and the rest, and break up their ancient herb garden?'" Hollis tapped the page. "Did you hear that? He said, 'What right had I to take away their herb garden?' I don't hear anything about traps. There you have it, right from HDT's mouth."

"All right," she finally said. "No traps, but can you find a way to bait them away from the cabin?" She lifted out a ravaged package of cookies. "Meanwhile, I'll try to find a mouse-proof pantry."

"No problem," he replied confidently. If he could feed the birds, why not the mice? Hollis gathered up his field glasses and sketchbook and was almost out the door, when a peculiar sound floated up from the Old Grove.

"Voices," he whispered.

We all strained to hear the distant ring of laughter. No one moved. We became forest animals who know their best defense is utter stillness.

"I can see the chimney," one voice said.

"This has to be it," another added. Boots sloshed up the slope to the cabin.

"How wonderful! It looks like a cottage in a fairy tale."

"Should we knock?" One of them lightly tapped the door. Hollis looked at us. They sounded harmless.

Go ahead, I motioned, and Hollis opened the door to Janice and Marjorie from our sixth-period English class.

"Hello! I hope we're not bothering you," Janice began. "We were just, well, we wanted to see Wayburn Woods and your cabin for ourselves."

We answered Janice by backing up against the walls to give them room to enter. They ignored the chairs we offered and sat on the floor. They happily sipped their tea, ate some stale crackers the mice hadn't invaded, and in every way enjoyed the cabin.

They also had a genuine interest in my column, which astonished me to no end. "We always read 'Notes from the Woods' first," Janice confided. "My dad asks me for the *Pine Press* every week just to read your article."

"He does? Really? Tell him thanks for me," I said.

And they had endless questions. How exactly did Rachel discover the uses of acorns? Where did we go in the green canoe? Did we often spend the night in the forest? How did Hollis become such a bird expert? Hollis grew so confident he offered to tour them through the feeding stations.

Rachel and I went along but hung back so that he could show off his birds in private. It was a treat to feel the sun on our shoulders and be dazzled by its reflection off the snow. I looked back at the cabin and could hardly distinguish it from the forest. Dark with moisture and moss, it did look like something out of a Hansel and Gretel woods.

We didn't know what to think when we first heard Hollis's bloodcurdling screams. Evidently Janice and Marjorie didn't either, because they began to scream too, without knowing why. Rachel and I scrambled up behind them but saw nothing. Hollis was livid.

"Squirrels!" he spat out. "They were swarming the feeder. It's hanging by a thread!" The garbage-can lid hung by one loop of clothesline, empty of seeds and squirrels. Above us in the limbs of the oaks, three or four squirrels sat motionless.

"You greedy jerks!" he called out.

Not so much as a whisker twitched. Rachel and I were used to Hollis's emotional outbursts where birds were concerned, but Janice and Marjorie must have been bewildered. Yet when Hollis stormed the slope to check the other stations, Janice was the first to fall in behind him with clenched fists.

"They're raiding all the stations! There's a whole army of them!" he shouted.

The squirrels flipped their tails and cackled, gorging their cheeks with sunflower seeds. Hollis finally resorted to throwing sticks, and they backed away grudgingly. At the last feeder Hollis shimmied up the trunk and scooted out onto the curved limb that held the feeder.

"They took it all. Only the millet is left and not much of that." He stirred the seed around in the tray. "It looks like mice have been in here too."

Rachel smiled smugly.

Janice was indignant; she didn't like injustice in any form. "Something should be done about this!" she kept saying.

Marjorie, however, wasn't coping well with all the screaming and running around. With the hood of her brown parka pulled tightly around her face, she looked like a frightened mouse herself.

We took a shortcut back to the cabin so that Hollis wouldn't have to see the feeders again. The squirrels had vanished, probably sleeping off the seed feast. The birds, though, were in full voice when Marjorie and Janice left us and headed up the old path.

"You're lucky those garbage-can lids have worked this long; after all, it's winter, for heaven's sakes, and the competition for food is fierce." Rachel was heating up a can of vegetable soup and tapped her spoon sharply on the pan. "And it's going to get worse; just wait until February, when the squirrels will be really hungry. I think you should do some research, find a feeder where only birds will be served."

"Meanwhile, they're starving," he said.

She poured him a cup of soup. "Not necessarily. These birds thought they could sustain themselves here. That's why they didn't migrate. Remember, they didn't have you last winter."

"No, but I've fed them all through autumn, and they're counting on me to feed them all winter too."

"You could be right," she said, licking the spoon. "Better get busy and design a new restaurant. When you're ready, come see my dad."

That night I wrote a long and flattering description of Janice Phelson and Marjorie Winfred, our first real guests in Wayburn. Then, feeling really bold, I dropped it off directly at the *Press* office the next day. I plopped the article down in front of Cindy Wedford, on top of the magazine she was reading, and said, "I want this in the next edition."

On Friday we discovered what good friends Janice and Marjorie really were. Janice wrote a full-page article about her appearance before the student council on Wednesday. She described the hungry birds she had seen and the attempts of Hollis Robbins to save them. Janice proposed that the student council make a thirty-dollar monthly donation to purchase seed for the birds of Wayburn Woods.

"At least until winter is over and the birds can find their own food, insects and so forth," she wrote. Janice noted that the council members seemed hesitant at first. I'll bet. Crepe paper, balloons, posters, and paints were the usual requests, things that went for entertaining the student body. But a donation for birds?

I guess there were some tense moments after Janice made her suggestion. Then Stuart Garfield got up. He wasn't an elected member of the council, but as editor of the *Press*, he had appointed himself as a consultant.

"This donation is not just for the birds," he began. "The students running this . . . sanctuary make valuable contributions to our school every week. Rachel Haygen has won an award for her study of plants, and Hollis Robbins has presented his slide show in our science classes. I've heard that his drawings have been sent to the Audubon Society. I think we owe them our support." He had left out my contribution, but that was okay.

I could have told Janice what would happen next. Stuart had so surpassed his classmates in the manipulation of student government that no one, not even the officers, dared to cross him. When Peter Torland, the president, asked, "All in favor of donating thirty dollars a month for the birds?" the measure passed by a landslide.

Janice wasn't satisfied, though. She went to the F&P on South Middleton and convinced the manager of the meat department to donate suet every week. Then she found a hardware store in Rockroad Harbor where they sold birdseed in large bags for a cheaper price. She even got a discount on top of that and set up a plan for Hollis's brother, Phil, to pick up the seed on his way home from work. Hollis could then tote it out to the woods, ten pounds at a time, in his knapsack, as he'd always done.

"I don't think Hollis realizes what an achievement this is," Rachel said to me on the bus ride home.

"Probably not," I said. "And can't you just see Janice organizing things like fund-raisers for the old folks' home and auctions for orphaned children someday?" She would carry a clipboard and be forever checking things off and making phone calls. She would see to it that things got done, things that were right and good.

Rachel said, "Anyone who can get the student council to subsidize birds can do anything. We're seeing genius at work."

Hollis was too involved with designing the new bird feeders to notice much else. Unfortunately, Rachel had used the word *restaurant* when she'd advised him, and Hollis had stuck with that idea. His final blueprint for the feeder was a platform that looked to me like a clumsy space station. Hollis explained that the design was based on the idea of choice.

"Each bird selects the seeds it wants—millet, hemp, flax, peanuts—and leaves the others alone," Hollis pointed out.

"Like a cafeteria," Rachel said.

"Exactly."

"And what are these?" she asked, pointing to a series of smaller containers around the central feeder.

"Those are for mixed seeds. Each one has six perches around it so that a group can eat together."

"Buffet or family style," she said.

"That's it! You see, it's all based on choice."

"No waiters? Bus birds to clean up the hulls? What about menus? Will reservations be needed?"

I gave her a warning look.

Mr. Haygen was more tactful when he looked the blueprint over some nights later. He rubbed his cheeks and squinted over the plan spread out on the Ping-Pong table. I didn't hear his words of rejection, but they must have been awfully gentle. In the end, they found a simple design in Thomas Haygen's Boy Scout handbook, and Hollis was happy with the results. They made eight of them in the basement and as many mesh baskets to hold the suet. I helped him cut and twist the thick wire that would suspend the feeders in midair, out of the reach of even the most skillful squirrel.

"Even if one tried to leap down on the lid," Hollis said from a high limb, "he couldn't reach the seed. He'd have to hang by his toes, and he still wouldn't make it."

One Sunday in January was spent loading Hollis's feeding stations with seed and fat. The chill in late afternoon hardened the slushy snow into jagged edges that caught our boots and made the downhill trail to the cabin treacherous.

We heard only the scrape of our boots and the clink of icy branches. Overhead the sky was smoothed over with snow clouds; by midweek a new layer of powder would cover our footprints and the sharp broken ice.

At the cabin we found Rachel making stew. She dropped spoonfuls of dumpling dough into the simmering pot. I sat cross-legged in an armchair and updated my journal. Hollis opened his sketchbook and resumed work on a fieldfare, but he looked up after a short while.

"That girl who got the money for the seed—" he began.

"Janice Phelson," I said.

"Right. I was thinking that I could write her a letter, you

know, and thank her. Maybe send her a drawing of the new feeders."

Rachel silently ladled stew into bowls and passed us some spoons.

"I think she'd like that," I said, and handed him some lined paper from my journal.

Hollis got at it right away, using the orange colored pencil he'd been drawing with. I started to suggest he use my pen instead, but didn't. Rachel and I sat back and watched the fire, eating our stew without talking so that he could concentrate. For the rest of the afternoon, the only sounds in the cabin were the steady strokes of his pencil.

Chapter 14

"I had three chairs in my house; one for solitude, two for
friendship, three for society. When visitors came in larger
and unexpected numbers, there was but the third chair for
them all, but they generally economized the room by
standing up."

H. D. THOREAU

Everybody found a path to our cabin in January. One Saturday three boys from school strolled into the clearing. They
snooped around with their hands jammed deep in their coats
and their ski caps pulled down low, for it was ferociously
cold. Soon they walked down to the frozen lake and disappeared from view.

"Do you know them, Beth?" Rachel asked.

"I think the short one is Mark Bitler. You remember
him—he carved a walking stick for his Henry project, but it
looked more like a golf club. The others I don't know."

The next weekend another group of boys showed up in
the Old Grove about ten in the morning. Hollis and I were

stacking wood behind the cabin when I recognized Larry Duncan's laugh and saw Ben Jones's stocky form leaping off the submarine tree into a drift.

They were curious about us, but didn't want to seem overly curious, and kept their distance, romping and hurling snow at one another on the borders of the grove. Two of them were molding snowballs into iceballs. Hollis feared his feeders would become targets, so he climbed the trail to keep an eye on them.

Larry and Ben waved. I walked up to meet them underneath the nest of the great horned owl.

"Has that goose ever come back?" Larry asked me.

Ben elbowed him and whispered, "Gort. Its name was Gort."

"Yeah, so is Gort still around?"

"No," I answered tentatively, unsure if they were teasing. "The Canada geese went south before the frost."

"That was great, the way you chased him in the canoe, and then jumped into the water to save him," Larry said with surprising sincerity.

"You should write more stories like that," Ben added. "That was your best one."

"It was *my* favorite, for sure." As Larry spoke, a snowball smashed into his back. Another clipped Ben's head, and spattered the three of us. Shouting threats and scooping up snow, they turned and chased their attackers back into the trees.

On Sunday we were again invaded. This time Janice led

a party of girls into the Old Grove and up to the cabin clearing. Rachel and I were inside and could hear them as they tiptoed noisily past the door.

Rachel groaned. "This is the trouble with accepting public funds; you have to accept the public."

All sorts of kids trickled into Wayburn Woods. Most of them just wanted a peek at the wild. I'm sure many were disappointed when they found nothing but a tiny dark cabin puffing out smoke and a few trails winding into the trees. We did our best to ignore them and went about our usual routine, but in a nervous, self-conscious way.

It might have been my fault. Henry wrote a chapter in *Walden* called "Winter Visitors"; I had written about Larry and Ben's visit and called the article "Rare Guests." I guess I made Larry and Ben look like daring explorers. Kids started seeing my article as an invitation, even a challenge to visit Wayburn. Not realizing I was setting off an avalanche, I kept on listing the students who showed up, and before I knew it, "Notes from the Woods" had become a sort of social column for the school. Readers rushed to the library to get their copies on Friday and skimmed my column to see who had been to the woods that week, whom they had gone with, and what they had done there. Incredible as it seemed, Wayburn Woods was becoming a place where popular kids went to be seen.

Rachel stayed in the cabin, kept the fire going, and read all the time now, mostly novels by Dostoyevsky. Wayburn was not the remote fortress she had once thought. At any moment Cindy Wedford could come marching up the slope with a troop of sharp-tongued girls under her command, and Rachel would be trapped.

"Look for Mrs. Stark to come skipping up here before you worry about Cindy," I said.

"Cindy will come," she said resignedly. "It's just a matter of time."

"Rachel, what could possibly interest Cindy out here? The view? The Old Grove? Hollis's bird feeders?"

"Revenge."

"What are you talking about?"

"The locker room. They'll never forget it, Beth. You invited them here. I know you were trying to help me. But you told them to come, and sooner or later they'll show up, and they'll be looking for me."

"I was taunting them! Did you think I was serious? Do you actually believe that they're just waiting to come get you, that they've been plotting against you all this time?"

Rachel did believe it. She believed that Cindy would not be satisfied until we were all humiliated as she had been, and the cabin was destroyed board by board.

"That's crazy, Rachel. You're overrating me; you're overrating all of us. We're no threat to Cindy Wedford, especially not the cabin."

Rachel wiped a circle in the steamy glass of the window and searched the hillside. "Yes, especially the cabin, Beth. Perhaps that's the biggest threat of all."

"Well, if they do show up and I'm not here, just pound

your pots and pans together and I'll come. Pound them with all your might—that is, if they haven't tied you up or something." But Rachel didn't think it was funny.

"Wayburn has upset the balance of power. You watch and see."

Meanwhile, the traffic in Wayburn Woods got worse, and the only person who didn't mind was Hollis. He saw most of it from the tops of trees anyway. Since the seed stations needed constant restocking, he now spent little time on the ground. His acrobatics sometimes drew small crowds and were accompanied by a lot of jingle-jangling because he wore a heavy belt around his waist to hold his ropes, tin pails, wire, and wire cutters. He and Stephen could hoist seed and suet up to the feeders in no time. Then Hollis would tumble out of the tree, sometimes dangling a few moments longer than necessary from a high branch, particularly if Janice was leading a tour.

These days I had to put up with constant company, not just at Wayburn but at home too. Mr. Louis McDuff was always in our living room with one eye on the television and the other on the newspaper, the sleeves of his dress shirt rolled up and his delicate, tasseled shoes resting across the coffee table. He was either on his way to the office or just returning from a meeting with investors.

Mother was a fully licensed agent now, and sold houses without any assistance. Mr. McDuff liked to plant himself in a comfortable chair so they could discuss the advantages of fixed interest rates over variables. He often stopped by around dinnertime with deli sandwiches or Blitz burgers. He taught me how to play chess and passed on to me his favorite bit of strategy.

"Beth, never hesitate to sacrifice something small to gain something larger," he said.

"You're just saying that because I'm taking one of your knights," I replied, whisking the black horse off the board.

"No, I'm saying it because you're not looking ahead, like I am."

I stared at the chess pieces but couldn't see very far into the future.

"Don't watch *your* men," he said quietly. "Watch mine and try to think like me." He touched the pointy hat of a harmless-looking bishop and studied me. I still didn't see the danger I was in.

"Think long range," Mr. McDuff said as he slid his bishop two spaces across the board.

I gasped. "My queen! She's—"

"Trapped," he said morbidly. "A victim of her own short-sightedness. Make sure that never happens to you, dear girl."

Mother and Mr. McDuff accepted my comings and goings without many questions, and since I usually carried my journal, they assumed I was off on some school-related activity with that studious-looking Haygen girl. I now used "going to Rachel's" to cover every excursion to Wayburn. Stephen was on guard at all times for any urgent summons home that my mother might telephone to the Haygens'. That would be his cue to take to the swiftest secret paths only he knew and bring me word in the woods.

No one was there to warn us of Stuart's next visit.

From the hill above the cabin, Rachel and I saw him, a black figure against the white forest. He cupped his hands and called out to the empty woods, "Anybody home?"

"Let him wait," Rachel whispered, crouching behind a tree.

"That doesn't seem nice," I said.

"He hasn't always been nice to us, Beth."

That didn't seem fair, either. Stuart had never been unkind to us. True, his newspaper had brought a lot of unwanted visitors out to Wayburn Woods, but it had also brought well-deserved recognition to Hollis and Rachel. I was now a published journalist thanks to the *Pine Press* and its editor in chief. Somehow we'd all gotten jumbled up with Stuart's ambition, and his impact on our lives wasn't easy to sort out, let alone judge.

"I'm going down," I said.

"Just be careful. He may be sniffing around for information."

"Rachel," I said, sighing.

He was searching the trails for us when I found him, and he seemed glad to see me. He handed me a gift, his celebrated map rolled up in a tube.

"You said once that it would look good hanging in the cabin," he said, "and now that the walls are plastered, maybe you can use some decoration."

"Thanks, Stuart."

I was glad Rachel wasn't there. She would have told him to keep his silly map so that he could find his way around the forest.

"Sorry I haven't been out here in a while. The paper keeps me busier than I could have imagined. And now the Winter Carnival is in full swing. I'm the coordinator and you wouldn't believe how much planning there is to do." As we walked the trails around the feeding stations, he told me about the booths and displays. Suddenly he stopped. "Would you come to the carnival, Beth?" he asked earnestly.

"Oh, I don't know," I said, so surprised that my legs felt wobbly on the snowy path. Was that why he'd come today—to ask me *that*?

He pulled a folded carnival flier from his pocket and gave me that too. "It'd be great to have you there. And I'm not the only one who thinks so. Lots of kids would like to meet the mysterious Beth Gardner who practically lives in the woods."

I was flabbergasted. Was he talking about my column? While I often thought about the kids who read "Notes from the Woods" every week, I'd never guessed they thought about *me*. At the clearing I considered asking Stuart into the cabin so we could sit by the fire. But I spotted Rachel's red knit cap popping up behind a snowdrift halfway down the slope. She'd never forgive me if I invited him inside.

"I'll look for you at the Winter Carnival," Stuart said before he left.

I wondered later what had happened to civil disobedience. I remembered when Stuart wanted us to follow our principles and do the right thing so that we would change the world. Now he was organizing dunking booths and ring toss games. Or maybe he was battling the one measly little injustice he could find. Until something more important came along, maybe the best he could do was to entertain us while we served out our term at Pine Brook Prison.

Chapter 15

"I weathered some merry snow storms, and spent some cheerful winter evenings by my fire-side, while the snow whirled wildly without, and even the hooting of the owl was hushed."

H. D. THOREAU

In late February Mr. McDuff announced that he was taking the entire Meadowcreek Hills office to Chicago for a week-long seminar, my mother included. The Haygens insisted that I stay with them. Mr. Haygen and Stephen picked me up in the Crestview Power Company truck on the evening before Mother left, so I could be settled in before school the next morning. Rachel rearranged her room, cleared off several shelves, and brought in a table where I could do my homework.

"Rachel, I'm only staying a week. I didn't bring any books or knickknacks."

"You'll need space," she said. "This is a big house, but

you're not used to so many people. You'll need a little place to call your own, even if it's empty."

I was glad that of all the places in the world, I was at the Haygens' when the big storm hit that week. Heavy snow began on Thursday night, and the Haygen kids, from six-year-old Grace to eighteen-year-old Kenneth, gathered soberly around the television weather report. The possibility of a snow day, a legitimate break from school, was approached as an almost religious event that could be ruined by premature celebration. We all slid to bed praying for a snowfall that would bury the snowplows and turn the school buses into helpless yellow whales, beached on the school yards.

When the news finally broke the next morning, we could hear hollering from every part of the house.

Middleton Road had been erased. We staggered into the street and lay down, making angels where the cars usually roared around the curve. The weekday had been choked. No cars, no buses, no offices, no schools—just kids rushing into a world of perfect snow.

There were endless discoveries to make in Wayburn, for ten inches of wind-driven snow collects around fallen trunks and hillsides in fantastic ways. Rachel, Hollis, and I ambled the morning away playing in a timeless white kingdom. Everything familiar was buried and cushioned out of recognition. This was new land, with no borders, where the great monster of school couldn't reach us.

Suddenly a woman, bundled up in a black car coat with a

fur-trimmed hood, rounded the turn from the Haygen path. She was smiling broadly.

Mr. Haygen appeared behind her. "Here we are!" he said. "Now you know where their hideaway is. Rachel!"

Rachel grabbed my sleeve and pulled me behind a tree. "Stark!" She clutched my arm.

"Mrs. Stark?"

"Rachel!" Mr. Haygen shouted. "You have a very special guest who's come a long way to see you!"

Rachel whispered, "Doesn't she know this is a day off?"

Mr. Haygen called again sharply.

As we walked up the slope, I felt we were climbing the stairs to her second-floor classroom, just like we did every day about this time. Mrs. Stark, however, acted as though we were throwing her a surprise party. She clapped her hands together as if we had just leaped out with Welcome banners.

"I am so glad I found you all! I *knew* this was where you would be on a day like today. Rachel, your father was so good to lead me out here." She turned to Mr. Haygen. "If not for him, I'd still be wandering along Middleton, looking for your cabin."

Now, there's a thought, Rachel conveyed with a glance of her eyes.

"Thank you, Mr. Haygen, I won't bother you anymore." She beamed at us. "I'm sure these three won't let me get lost. I'm with real forest-dwellers now."

Mr. Haygen was looking pleased again. After all, what

greater compliment than for a teacher to visit her students, especially in conditions like these.

"Is Rachel working hard at her studies?" he asked.

"Oh my, yes," Mrs. Stark said, admiring the sulky Rachel. "She's a joy to have, such a joy."

"We always watch their report cards, but you let me know if she ever starts to slip."

I couldn't imagine Rachel "slipping"; I had never known her to be motivated by grades or by a desire to please her parents; getting As in school was simply what Rachel did.

Mr. Haygen left, but he stopped several times on the path to see how the visit was going without his supervision.

Having Mrs. Stark thrust on us for the afternoon was an immense disappointment for Rachel and me, but for Hollis it was catastrophic. Rachel and I found Mrs. Stark a boring and sometimes unpleasant teacher, but we completed our work for her class and were rewarded with As. Hollis didn't finish half his assignments, and the few compositions he did turn in were awful. Mrs. Stark was generous when she doled out Ds to Hollis, and I think his close link to Rachel and me was the only reason she didn't flunk him.

"Where should we begin?" she asked.

"There's not that much to see," Hollis muttered, and gestured halfheartedly toward the cabin. "This is pretty much all there is."

"Now, I know that's not true. Why don't we start with your bird feeders, Hollis, and I'd like to see the Old Grove, the cabin, of course, and then I'd love to sample some of your famous forest cuisine!" She winked at Rachel. As always, she had an agenda for the day, as detailed and inflexible as the grammar-book pages she listed on the board.

We set out toward the feeders, following Mrs. Stark, who grew more agile and lively the farther we went into the woods. She did all the talking, just like in class, repeating all she knew about our projects in the woods and stopping only now and then to ask for our confirmation.

"So this is where you chased the squirrels away, is that right, Hollis?"

"Yeah."

"And down in this cove you still have acorns buried, don't you, Rachel?"

"Yes."

"You must be looking forward to the spring thaw, so you can pull them out."

"Yes."

"And Beth, I'll bet you never run out of things to write about with so many adventures at hand."

"No."

And on and on it went. On this day of magic and freedom, we were led around Wayburn like manacled slaves. When we completed the circle of paths that wound back up to the cabin door, we were almost fighting to do the few chores that would buy us some moments of escape. Hollis made a huge to-do about the need to fetch more firewood. We went together, loudly estimating how much digging it would take before we could even reach the tarp.

Under pressure from Mrs. Stark, who wanted "the full Wayburn experience," Rachel put the last of her acorn meal, which she had been saving for a special occasion, into a pan and made wilderness coffee. Hollis and I pulled down enough wood for the next two weeks and then crouched in the snow beside the woodpile to wait indefinitely, but Rachel wasn't about to stay alone with Mrs. Stark and rapped on the glass.

Once inside, we spent a lot of time getting everyone's cup of coffee flavored just right with milk and sugar. Then Mrs. Stark sat in the armchair and looked surprisingly content. Rachel told me later that it was the coffee that caused Mrs. Stark's transformation, the one we witnessed that afternoon. But I convinced her that potent as the acorns were, it was the beauty of the woods under white blankets that changed Dorothy Stark.

Mrs. Stark saw the copy of *Walden* on the TV tray, reached out, and laid her hand on it. She grew dreamy-eyed as she sipped her coffee and stared for a long time at the flames in the stove pit. We sat silently too, just as students do in class when a teacher pauses in an endless lecture.

"You have given me a lovely day, and I'll not ever forget it," she said in a voice very unlike her usual prattle. We knew that an equally kind response was due here, and it was Hollis who managed to deliver it. "We had a nice time too, Mrs. Stark."

"Thank you, Hollis. You know, I've never had students like you before." She studied him closely, and while this didn't sound too bad, I could see Hollis bracing himself for a run-down of his lazy ways. She looked warmly at his hair, sticking out like fresh straw from under his cap, and at the chart on the wall behind him of the Ones Who Stayed Behind.

"I have visited Walden Pond when I've stayed with my sister in Boston, and I have taught the excerpt from *Walden* in your literature books for many years, but nothing like this has ever come of it. I am so grateful to have shared in it." She paused again for another long while. "If I were young, if I were your age . . . oh how I would love to join you here in this pocket of wilderness that you have found." She laughed as if she could see herself, at fourteen years old, sitting with us on the cabin floor. Then she sat up, finished her coffee, and slowly rose.

"I know I have been a profound inconvenience to you all today, and I do thank you for showing me your . . . Walden. But now I must go and find my way home."

"You don't need to go so soon, Mrs. Stark," I heard myself saying. "We haven't even had anything to eat yet; Rachel can cook up something really quickly."

"Thank you, dear. No, I've a long walk ahead of me, but perhaps another time."

We led Mrs. Stark back to the Haygen house and even halfway to Hawthorn Lake, searching as we went for ways to ease our guilt about not giving her a friendlier welcome. Rachel and I suggested a canoe trip for her next visit.

"After the trees bud and the mayapples bloom," Rachel said.

Before we parted, Mrs. Stark turned to us. "I must say, I

am surprised that your fourth partner didn't join us today, but maybe on my next visit."

"You mean Stuart?" I asked.

"Of course."

Stuart hadn't been to the woods since he invited me to the carnival. I hadn't gone to his lavish event, nor had I seen him much at school. Who knew what project now occupied his time.

The sun had come out, and I squinted back at Mrs. Stark through the glare. I wanted to explain that Stuart would probably not be at the cabin the next time she visited, or maybe even ever again, but she had walked away. She waved to us, and somewhere in the distance we heard the low drone of a snowplow working its way up Middleton. We hurried back to the cabin to enjoy the last three hours of daylight and the last hard grip of winter in the woods.

Chapter 16

"The mass of men lead lives of quiet desperation."
H. D. THOREAU

We talked about spring long before it arrived. All through the slushy month of March we talked, mostly holed up in the cabin. Henry said in spring, "Walden is melting apace," and now we knew what he meant. We didn't need the warmth or music of the fire stove anymore; the air was only faintly cool and was filled with a racket of splashing and gushing from streams in every direction.

"Good thing we set the wall boards deep in the ground, or we might need oars pretty soon," Hollis said.

The cabin actually flooded one day when rains brought down a wash of leaves and silt from the hillside. Below us, on the slope to the Old Grove, a row of miniature waterfalls chattered and ran, sounding so much like showers that often we were fooled into opening the door. "Is it raining again?" we'd complain, only to find that it wasn't rain but snowmelt from the entire forest above us, dividing into a thousand eddies, vying for space to tumble down.

Wayburn was budding and sprouting all over the place, and Rachel finally woke up from her long hibernation in the cabin. She put on tall fisherman's boots and waded into the inlet where the cattail shoots were poking up between the dried leaves of the year before. She patrolled the banks for arrowhead, miner's lettuce, wild onion, and milkweed.

"I was such an amateur last year," she said. "This spring, I'll harvest early and we'll sample real forest cuisine."

Hollis and I hoped that Rachel wouldn't find some of these special weeds. We were perfectly happy with the canned food we'd eaten all winter, but Rachel was adamant.

"Soon we'll have wild onion soup and cossack asparagus, baked swamp potatoes and sumac tea."

"Swamp potatoes? Do me a favor and don't tell me any more about them," Hollis said.

"They're not as obnoxious as they sound. Lewis and Clark ate them. The Indians showed them how."

"How do you know the Indians weren't just trying to discourage them from exploring the wilderness? Having to eat swamp potatoes sounds to me like a good excuse to go home."

"Well, we may have to wait awhile," Rachel said. "None have come up in the inlet, but maybe later . . . across the lake."

"And cossack asparagus?" I asked.

"They wear little fur hats and dance on the vines," Hollis added, his colored pencil working across the paper.

"Those are easy; they're the first foot or so of the cattail stalks."

"I can hardly wait," he said.

And we didn't have to wait long. As soon as the young shoots sprang up, she peeled them and crunched down on them solidly.

"They're like cucumbers," she instructed us. And when the greenish yellow flower stems started up, she husked them like corn, boiled them, buttered them, and made us eat them.

"You see this little tidbit here?" She pointed to the base of the stem. "That's the real gem, just like a potato." And, of course, we ate that too.

"What will this do to us?" Hollis asked. "How do you know it won't have some permanent effect?"

"It's a little late to worry about that," Rachel answered, and went right on squeezing nutrition from every inch of the cattails.

Wayburn grew so green and dense that one day I couldn't see the Old Grove or the inlet from the cabin, so shaggy was the undergrowth. The thickening moss on the tree trunks absorbed our voices. Hollis couldn't hear me anymore when I shouted for him from the cabin. Wayburn was soft and dappled. Leaves and vines were tumbling into our pathways, pressing against the sides of the cabin, and crawling up and over our shingled walls and roof.

As the forest warmed, Hollis was gradually freed from

the feeding stations. The student council still bought the seed and Hollis still hauled it to the cabin, but the urgent need was over. Clouds of gnats hovered in the shade; the ground wriggled with larvae. Now he had time to draw and record his first sightings. He mapped out their nests and told us where we should walk to avoid disturbing the households of blue jays and flickers. The migratory birds were back, and the Ones Who Stayed Behind had lots of company again. Even our old friends the Canada geese landed in the inlet one morning.

"Do you suppose Gort is with them?" I asked Hollis. The geese foraged in the shallow, weedy water, while he considered.

"He'll probably avoid Wayburn Lake, remembering the minnow net and all. If he does come back, I think I'll recognize him," he finally said. "Gort will definitely know me."

In spring it was obvious that all the birds knew Hollis. His love for the birds was well known, but their affection for him became our own private wonder. I thought at first that it was the seed that drew them to Hollis, until a time I saw him sitting against the submarine tree with only his sketch pad. Several black-capped chickadees hopped around his feet, then up onto his knees and shoulders. He opened up his writing hand and a small male jumped in and pecked about in his palm, perched on his fingertips, and hopped along his wrist. He never talked to us about it, probably because it had become so common.

I got a good look at Hollis in the spring after he had shed the bulky pea coat and knit cap he'd worn all winter. He had grown three inches, passing up Rachel and me. His face had lengthened and become more angular, his shoulders had broadened, and the twitchy nervousness in his legs was gone. I helped him repair shingles on the cabin roof and wondered if he was beginning to look like his older brother, Phil, the one we'd never seen except from a distance in the school parking lot.

Hollis sure didn't resemble the restless boy who had joined our group for the Experiment in Living. I couldn't tell if he resembled his mother, because I had seen her only once when Mother was driving me to school. As we passed his house I saw a car turning into their driveway off Middleton. I couldn't tell if she had Hollis's straight yellow hair or blue-green eyes. Like Phil, she was a faceless, shadowy figure, and it was hard to imagine her as Hollis's mom.

When Hollis didn't appear at school or the cabin for over a week, Rachel convinced me that we should pay a visit to the Robbinses' house. I wasn't sure we should just show up there; Hollis never mentioned his family, never even hinted at an invitation. Around his home life ran a barbed wire fence, and we had always respected it.

"It's the neighborly thing to do," Rachel said.

"He's not our neighbor, Rachel, he's our friend."

"All the more reason we should find out if he's still alive—that's the friendly thing to do. Besides, he's *my* neighbor."

We brought Stephen along so it might look as though the visit was his idea. "His mom won't be there," Rachel calculated, "but we'll probably meet Phil and maybe some of his friends from the Drexter factory. Phil's shift starts at seven, so we'll get to see what they do in the afternoon."

"How do you know all this?" I asked.

Stephen looked uncomfortable when Rachel ignored my question. "I know Tommy Wyndon," he said. "He lives next door and sees a lot at the Robbinses'."

"I see. That's just great, Rachel, having your little brother spy on Hollis. It's pretty clear that he doesn't want us to meet his family. We should leave him alone."

"It's time he got over it. We're his best friends, his only friends—who better to help him?"

"Help him what? I don't see that he needs any help," I said.

"I guess we'll know about that soon enough."

We headed up the Robbinses' dirt driveway to the dingy summer cottage that seemed large enough to hold at most two or three rooms. The porch was warped and unswept and held a single rusting lawn chair. Rachel was already knocking on the screen door.

"Yeah?" Almost immediately Phil Robbins stood in the shade of the doorway.

"I'm Rachel Haygen and we're friends with Hollis. We haven't seen him in a while and we were wondering if he was all right."

"He's got the flu. He's okay," Phil said, taking a sip from a soda can.

Rachel put her face up to the screen, peering in. "Well, we'd like to talk to him."

Phil took a few more swigs and seemed to be deciding whether or not to reply. "He's asleep. I'll tell him you came by." Without so much as a nod, he retreated into the house.

"Excuse me!" Rachel called through the door. "I'm sure Hollis would like to see us. We have his homework assignments!" Her nose was almost flattened on the screen.

"Rachel! Come on, let's get out of here." I was certain Phil's manners wouldn't be changed much by the mention of homework.

"Hollis, are you all right?" Rachel poked her head inside. "Hollis? Are you awake?" Then she slipped through the murky doorway of the Robbinses' house. Stephen ran up the steps and slid in behind her before the door could bang shut. I didn't want to be left alone in that dreary yard, so I jumped onto the porch and followed them in.

For a few minutes I couldn't see much of the dark interior. I gradually distinguished Phil sitting on a shabby sofa bed with the bedding all askew; he was watching television with the volume turned down to a murmur.

We followed Rachel down a narrow hallway to the kitchen, and there, barefoot on the peeling linoleum, stood Hollis in a wrinkled undershirt and sweat pants.

"Hi," he said huskily.

"Hey, Hollis," Stephen answered.

"We were worried about you," I said.

He looked embarrassed, but as he tried to speak, a cough clattered into his throat. His hair was flattened on his forehead and dark with perspiration; his eyes were glassy. Rachel reached out and put her hand on his forehead.

"You've got at least a hundred and two or three," she said firmly. "Have you taken any aspirin?"

"I'm fine. My mom made me stay home all week, but I'm really fine. She's a nurse, you know." His voice seemed to come from far away, as if he'd not quite returned from a long journey.

"I bet you haven't eaten anything today. You look as skinny as Stephen. What have you had?"

Without waiting for a reply, Rachel opened cupboards and clanged around, digging into the refrigerator and shaking boxes of crackers. I stole a quick look around the kitchen, not wanting to stare at its awful poverty. There was a table and some folding chairs, but otherwise the room was bare—not a curtain, not a cookie jar, nothing. Above the table a large section of the wall had been cut away as if with a hatchet, and the supporting boards showed through like ribs. I looked down to see Stephen's reaction. His house was such a colorful hodge-podge of toys and hardware and wild chases around the Ping-Pong table. What would he think of this war-torn kitchen and the sullen older brother who stared vacantly into a muttering TV?

Phil came and leaned against the doorjamb, still sipping his soda and taking in the scene with no more interest than he had the television. He watched Rachel heat up some soup and force Hollis into eating at the table. He wore shapeless blue work pants and a shirt with the Drexter emblem on the pocket, but he reminded me of the rough high school boys with tattooed arms who hung around the bowling alley in Rockroad Harbor wearing low-slung pants.

Hollis was obediently eating his chicken noodle soup. "There is one thing you could do," he said weakly. "My brother picked up the seed last week. He could take it out to the cabin and you could fill the feeders. The nights are still pretty cold, and I think the sparrows miss it."

That's how we ended up returning to Wayburn in Phil's old Camaro, the Flying Devil.

"We shouldn't take Stephen in that car, Rachel," I said to her while we waited outside. "It seems to me that this is getting into a car with a stranger."

"It'll be fine. He shouldn't walk back along the road alone anyway."

"Then let's walk back and meet Phil at your house," I said.

"No, I haven't seen enough yet."

He turned out to be a cautious driver, and the Flying Devil pulled into the Haygens' driveway without any screeches or death-defying turns. Phil lifted two forty-pound sacks of seed over his shoulder and took the shortcut to the cabin door without any guidance at all.

He never said a word, just went in the cabin, looked around, and tried the latch on the window. Before he left, he walked up the path to the feeders and stood for a while with his hands on his hips. I thought he was arrogant and dangerous-looking.

"Like a grown-up delinquent," I said to Rachel after he'd gone.

School became an agony for us by late April. Ever since the icebound lakes had broken into a choppy blue, everyone was fidgety. But for Rachel, Hollis, and me, it was unbearable torture. Nothing could substitute for Wayburn Woods—not baseball practice, not the tennis team, not the Sadie Hawkins Dance, not the new spring clothes from Glamma Girl. We had to spend seven hours a day missing the swift changes in the woods. In seven hours loons could land on the lake and depart unseen, honey could rise and fall in the stems of red clover, dragonflies could live a lifetime.

When Hollis had recovered from the flu, he and Phil patched up the leaks in the green canoe; then we all helped with the portage from Hawthorn Lake to Wayburn Lake, where we launched it from the inlet.

Sundown came well after six o'clock, so we went on trips to the end of the lake to watch Mr. Wayburn's cows graze by the water. *When school is out* became our favorite phrase; it opened nearly every conversation we had in the woods. We were like old misers counting our gold every day, except we added up the days and weeks of summer vacation. We greedily estimated how far our wealth would take us in the canoe and up the wooded banks of the land that bordered the lake.

"I think we should begin here," Hollis said, pointing out

the sandy stretch of beach at the lake's northernmost tip. "We could hide the canoe in the weeds and set up a base camp behind those trees. Then we could hike into the hills."

"How far?" Rachel asked.

"Until we run out of supplies, or until we find a road or a house."

"We won't run out of supplies," Rachel said. "How many times do I have to say it—by midsummer the forest will be a supermarket! Even you will be able to find three meals a day."

This was an old argument that could last the length of the lake. We never talked about how we would get away from our families for that long. We weren't bothered by anything realistic. That's what months of reading Henry will do for you. We concentrated instead on the bigger problems of bug repellent and camping gear.

But May brought changes to Wayburn Woods. Some were slight; some were skyscrapers. Mother's announcement that she and Mr. McDuff were to be married was not a surprise. I had been expecting it since Valentine's Day, when he had given her a garnet ring inside a heart-shaped box of candy. For me there was a smaller box with a dainty ID bracelet engraved with my initials.

I liked Mr. McDuff just fine, his gifts notwithstanding. I liked the way he made my mother laugh, and the way he read editorials in the Sunday paper aloud and then asked me my opinion. I liked the way he ordered for me at Blitz's, saying, "The lady will have a cheeseburger." I liked the way he and

Mother kept so busy and involved with the real estate office that they never noticed how often I was "going to Rachel's."

I concluded that the marriage would not interrupt my life in the woods. That is, until I learned that we would be moving, not just to a different house, but to a different part of town. Our banishment was over. We were returning to Meadowcreek Hills, my mother's Promised Land.

Mother explained that our life with Louis would give me all sorts of advantages. That might have meant something to me back in the fall before I'd met Henry, before we had started our experiment in the woods. But it was too late now. The wedding was set for late autumn, when the Michigan real estate market had passed its peak. I would have one summer in Wayburn before miles of highway and endless suburbs came between us.

We should have recognized the other signs of trouble sooner, but it was hard to see anything threatening in Wayburn that spring. Stephen's sharp eyes spotted the first one, on the three-tiered hill, a small yellow flag flying from a stake in the ground. Then we started seeing them everywhere: by the Haygen path, several hundred yards east of the inlet, on the ridge above the Old Grove.

"Somebody's been here! What are those things?" Hollis asked.

"They're markers," Rachel replied.

"Markers, for what?" Hollis asked.

"How should I know!"

"Maybe Mr. Wayburn is going to drill for oil," he guessed.

"Right. Michigan is full of oil wells," Rachel said.

"Or maybe he's going to bring some of his cows over here to graze. Maybe he's putting up a fence."

"Cows in the forest?" she said dryly.

"Not the forest, the meadow—you could graze cows there."

Rachel stopped stripping the bark off a sassafras root and thought about it. "Maybe . . . you could be right. It's for the cows," she said.

Rachel and Hollis were too innocent to know what those markers meant. I'd seen them plenty of times before at model home sales, where new houses sat on the bleak remains of fields and forests. Those cheery yellow flags were survey markers, the tombstones of trees. They showed where one lot ended and another began, like stickers the butcher slaps onto cut-up meat so the buyer knows what part of the animal he's getting. But I didn't say anything. I pretended it was cows and not the onslaught of subdivisions that was on the way.

On Memorial Day we dragged a bushel basket of Rachel's acorns from the lake. It took all of us to haul it to the beach. Rachel untied the gunnysack and let Hollis and me have the first look inside. The acorns were rich black and smelled of fresh water.

"They look good enough to eat," Hollis said.

"And so we shall," Rachel said regally. "So we shall."

She was still rinsing them off at the shoreline when Stephen appeared on the ridge above us, winded and frightened.

"You better come see this," he said. We walked up the Haygen path and almost out of the woods without seeing anything that could have scared him. But at the trailhead, only twenty feet or so from Middleton, a large rectangle had been set securely into the ground. The top was curved in a familiar curlicue, but the front was covered with words whose shape and meaning were as foreign as a hieroglyph:

SOLD:

400 ACRES LAKE-VIEW PROPERTY

Future site

of

WAYBURN MANOR ESTATES

LUXURIOUS LAKESIDE HOMES

McDUFF REALTY

Chapter 17

"I left the woods for as good a reason as I went
there. Perhaps it seemed to me that I had several
more lives to live, and could not spare any
more time for that one."
H. D. THOREAU

"Mr. McDuff . . . Isn't that your mom's friend, Beth?" Hollis
asked.

"Her new stepfather," Rachel said.

"Not yet," I said. "He's not my stepfather yet." And if
I had anything to do with it, he never would be. All the way
home I mentally tossed away every gift Mr. McDuff had ever
given me. It took a while too, because I realized that he had
woven himself into my life pretty securely.

Mr. McDuff and my mother were having cocktails in
our living room and listening to some Latin music on the
stereo when I walked in. Louis was slumped in his over-
stuffed chair, and his feet, as always, were on the coffee table.

"You're back early, Beth," Mr. McDuff crooned. "You girls studying for finals?"

"What difference would it make," I said curtly.

Mother looked up. "Is something wrong?" she asked.

"Yes, there's something wrong, I'd say. McDuff Realty has just sold all of Wayburn Woods and it's about to be turned into a house factory."

"Wayburn Woods . . . ," Mother said. "Louis, isn't that the large development off Middleton?"

"Yes, Lakeland Construction. Escrow closed back in January."

"You've known all this time and never said anything?" I asked.

Mr. McDuff straightened up in the chair. "Beth, before you go casting blame, I think you'd better get all the facts first."

"I know one fact—the name of your real estate company is on that sign!"

"Beth, I will *not* have you speaking this way!" Mother set her drink down and rose from the sofa.

"It's all right, Isabel. I'll deal with this," he said.

"You 'deal' everything, don't you? Is there anything you wouldn't sell? Is there anything?"

"Beth!" my mother shouted.

"Let me tell you about that farm, Beth. The Wayburns once owned most of this township. There were at least four or five lakes included in the original boundaries, and they've been shaving off parcels and selling them for decades. They have to; the property taxes are killing them. This latest four hundred acres is only a fraction of the land. Granted, that acreage is probably some of the most beautiful and accessible. The homes along that ridge, once it's cleared, will be worth a fortune! But there will be plenty of forest left for a hundred years to come."

"I don't care if Eugene Wayburn wants to sell it! Neither of you has a right to destroy that forest! You're thieves! Both of you!"

Mother couldn't have looked more frightened if I had been swinging a baseball bat into her cabinet of fine china, and in a way, I guess I was. I ran up the stairs before either of them could respond.

I paced around my room, shaking, unable to sit down.

Spring had made me lazy. For the last three issues I'd filled up "Notes from the Woods" with Henry's poems that I'd copied from the back of *Walden,* and wild edible recipes by Rachel Haygen. Only one more issue of the *Press* would be published, and it would be filled with honor roll lists and popularity polls telling us who had the cutest smile and who was most likely to succeed. I had one last shot. All winter long kids had read about Wayburn Woods; some even knew the way there and had walked its paths. Now they needed to know that Wayburn was going to be plowed under and paved over. I stayed up most of the night writing a last article. I called it "Death of a Forest."

They started tearing up Wayburn just two days later. A forty-ton bulldozer cut a wide strip along the edge of the woods, parallel to Middleton; it took out most of the staghorn sumac that ringed the forest on the roadside. Then the bulldozer lunged into the trees, checking the softness of the soil, we supposed, to see where the real butchery would begin. One of these lunges took out the first thirty or forty feet of the Haygen path; another one lifted a group of young birches out of the dirt and their roots were drying slowly in the sun. A building pad was cleared farther down, close to the three-tiered hill, where trailers could be set up, equipment stored, and fencing installed.

By the time we arrived after school, the engine had cooled and the forest was strangely quiet.

"Listen," Hollis said. "The tanagers have gone."

We walked the length of the gash in silence. The forest had been cut open, boldly and intentionally, as if a surgeon had made his first incision. We'd never seen Wayburn Woods wounded. We'd never seen the deep, black layer of soil that ran underneath everything like a river. Our shoes sank into it. We breathed it in. It had taken hundreds of years to form and less than an afternoon to bleed out.

I didn't stay long at the cabin. I was too much of a coward, too afraid that I'd see some other atrocity lying around the next turn. Rachel went down to the shoreline to look for her arrowhead plant. Hollis sketched a flicker from the cabin clearing. I had nothing to write about. The changes in Wayburn were already too big to talk about, the future too horrible to imagine.

Rachel phoned me that night. "Can you talk?" she asked.

"Of course I can talk."

"Well, I just thought that"—her voice trailed off to a whisper—"Mr. McDuff might be there."

"What?"

"Mr. McDuff!"

"No, he's gone, for tonight."

"Stuart came to the cabin after you left. He thinks he can save Wayburn."

I'd always admired Stuart's intelligence and ambition. I admired more things about Stuart than I liked to admit, but I wasn't in the mood for this.

"Rachel, the deal is done. They're going to build a subdivision in Wayburn Woods and not even Stuart Garfield can change that."

"I think we should listen to him. He wants to be our . . . agent."

"Our *agent*?"

"He has ideas, Beth."

"Stuart always has ideas."

"He's also done research. Stuart says the real villain is the developing company, Lakeland Construction. He thinks that with public exposure and student support, Lakeland could be pressured into giving up the project. He says it's the ultimate battle between good and evil."

Evidently Rachel had forgotten how much she disliked Stuart. She'd forgotten all about his "pushy" editorials and his "bossy" attitude around school.

"So if he becomes our agent," I asked, "what then? What do we have to do?"

"Nothing. He says we should be prepared for a little attention is all."

"What kind of attention?"

"He didn't say specifically."

The next morning I discovered that Stuart's new role as our agent was well under way. After the morning announcements in homeroom, Stuart addressed the entire school over the PA system: "Listen up, all Pine Brook students. A special edition of the *Pine Press* will be issued today. It is vitally important that each of you read it carefully. Your future, the future of our planet, may depend on it."

From there, the attention that Stuart hinted of detonated like a missile. I was called to the principal's office during third period to explain how my column "Death of a Forest" had ended up on the editorial pages of the *Detroit Free Press* and the *Detroit News*. It came as a surprise to me as well. I had never in my life been summoned to the principal's office, and I waited anxiously while Mr. Putterman drummed his fingers on the newspapers.

"I see that you and your friends, Hollis Robbins and Rachel Haygen, have developed an ongoing science project out in Wayburn Woods. Is that correct?" He underlined their names on a notepad.

"Not exactly," I said. He looked at me through his thick glasses, reminding me of an aging raccoon.

"What kind of project is it, then?" he asked suspiciously.

"It's part science and part . . . philosophy."

"Is it part of your philosophy to trespass on private property?"

"Yes. I mean, we knew Mr. Wayburn owned it, but we had his permission."

"I see," he said. "May I ask whose idea it was to send this essay of yours to Detroit's major newspapers?"

I almost said it was my agent's idea but decided not to. "It was my idea, sir."

"And did you ever consider consulting with an adult and getting permission before submitting this to a public forum?"

"No, I didn't."

"Uh-huh." He stared at me through those black circles. "Your letter is impertinent. These 'demonic developers,' as you call them—are you aware that they are prominent people in our community? Did it ever occur to you that this might place your school in a bad light?"

"No, I never thought of that."

"You have embarrassed me, Miss Gardner. You have embarrassed yourself and your school. I am simply confounded that you didn't bring this situation to my attention before you exposed it to the city!"

I had never met Mr. Putterman before, not up close. I'd seen him from my seat in the bleachers at award assemblies and pep rallies, but he was no more approachable to me than was the president of the United States. I couldn't think of a polite way to explain that he would be the *last* person on earth in whom I would confide anything.

"Well, you have put me in an extremely awkward position, extremely awkward."

I was dismissed and ordered back to class.

The morning was bad, but it was nothing compared to what the *Pine Press* unleashed that afternoon when student council members passed it out at every exit door. They stuffed the new issue into each student's hand, along with the whispered slogan: "Save Wayburn Woods."

The end-of-the-year accolades and much-looked-for popularity poll results were gone. The entire first page was devoted to the sale of Wayburn Woods, and Stuart Garfield, editor and now agent, had gone mad with headlines:

Science Project Sacrificed to Ruthless Developers

Bulldozers Plow Up Paradise

Thoreau's Ideals Subdivided

Who Will Save the Birds?

My column was in its usual space, but it paled beside the other articles. Stuart had written most of them, though Janice Phelson, champion of the winter birds, had written one. "We fed the birds of Wayburn and helped them survive through horrible snowstorms," she wrote. "Now those same birds will see their trees and nests cut down. These are not just any birds; they are *our* birds, and we must fight to save them!"

Was it the hundreds of tiny bird eyes forced to watch the chainsawing of the forest, or was it the thirty dollars the treasurer paid out every month for birdseed that ignited the student council? Not even Janice knew for sure. But she had given the twenty-five homeroom representatives something to care about during the last monotonous months of school, and they were keen on setting the whole school ablaze with Wayburn Woods fever.

"Beth!" Someone shouted my name, and I turned to see Stuart running from the front doors, where he'd been handing out the *Press*. He held a hefty stack under his arm.

"Have you seen it?" he asked.

"You gave us the whole front page," I said.

"Are you kidding? You've got the whole paper! But the best part is . . ." He flipped his pile of papers over and showed me the back page of the *Press*. "The 'Action Guide' is where kids choose how they want to protest the development of Wayburn Woods. See, there are three levels—"

"Are you sure everybody wants to protest?" I interrupted.

"How could they *not* protest something so unfair? Now those who are really fired up can collect signatures on petitions. And look, here's the address and telephone number of the mayor, so anyone who wants can call him or write letters. Finally, for all the other kids, there's Green Day. That's where we all wear green as a statement against the destruction of Wayburn Woods. What do you think?"

I honestly didn't believe many students would care enough to follow his "Action Guide," but I was impressed that he cared enough to write it.

"I think it's a terrific idea, Stuart, and I hope you're right," I said.

"I knew you'd like it." He smiled. "Henry David Thoreau is written all over it." He looked proudly down at the "Action Guide" and read to me what I'm sure was his favorite sentence. "'Read this guide and put your *CONSCIENCE* into *ACTION*!'"

My bus was closing its doors, and I had to hurry away to catch it. I flopped into the seat Rachel had saved for me.

She had her nose deep in the middle pages of the *Press*, but on the way home she filled me in on what *wasn't* written in the newspaper.

"Green Day is not what it appears to be," she told me. "On the surface it's about wearing green clothes, but the real meaning of Green Day is something else entirely."

We slid down in our seats for more privacy.

"Green Day is going to be a student walkout," she continued.

"You mean like a *strike*?" I asked. She nodded ominously.

Approval for Green Day slid right past the adult sponsors. They didn't know that students were planning to stampede out of the school in their green outfits. They believed this little protest would be no more disruptive than our annual Pajama Day. So while Green Day banners were hung on walls all over campus, the Green Day *Walkout* announcement was unofficially spread by word of mouth, and within a day every student was in on it.

At home a quiet truce had settled over the three of us. Mr. McDuff stopped by throughout the day and evening as always, a little preoccupied with business, but otherwise rock-steady and cheerful again. Mother pretended that nothing unusual had happened between Mr. McDuff and me. Only an elaborate roast beef dinner she cooked on Tuesday indicated that our quiet routine had been shaken at all. I brought up the subject of Wayburn when Mother was cleaning up the dishes, hoping to show Mr. McDuff that I didn't hold any grudges.

"This Lakeland Construction Company, what will they do next?" I asked.

He looked surprised. "There will be more detailed surveying first. My guess is they'll be putting up about five hundred houses initially, good-size ones on at least a quarter of an acre; splitting it up will take a few more weeks."

"How many houses will there be when it's all done?"

He exhaled loudly. "About sixteen hundred eventually, but it will take a few years before they complete all the phases, and they'll probably complete the golf course before they begin the last phase."

"So what happens after the surveying is done?"

"Grading, smoothing, and leveling the land, making pads for the foundations." He paused to see if I really wanted to hear the gory details. I did.

"The ridge above the lake will probably be scraped and widened, and most of the soil will go down into the bowl below, into that big clump of trees."

"The Old Grove," I said.

"Much of that will be covered in fill, lessening the angle of the slope to the lake."

"Will they cut down all the trees?"

"No, Lakeland's a smart outfit with big money behind it. They'll be willing to pay for the special handling of some of those old trees. They won't take out all of them, Beth, but most will have to go; otherwise construction costs would make the whole venture unprofitable."

"When will it start, the grading and cutting?"

"Very soon, I'd imagine. I'm sure they'll want the models for the first phase framed and roofed by early fall."

"So they could start anytime now, cutting down the trees," I said.

"Yes, they could," he said gently.

Rachel brewed the first wilderness coffee of the season with grim determination.

"It will be much better than last year's, I can promise you that. After a winter in the lake, the acorns will be much sweeter, and who knows, over the years we can try all kinds of places." She handed me a cup so vigorously, it splashed over the sides. She set another one down by Hollis.

"Rachel, we have to talk about something," I said.

"If you don't want to go to all that trouble, it's okay. We

can just drag the bushel basket into the inlet again. Anyway, how is it?"

"It's not that. The coffee's delicious. I want to talk about the cabin and Henry."

"Why do you want to talk about that? It's not over, if that's what you're getting at. Stuart's plan is going to work. Everyone at school is talking about it. My dad even said that a foreman at the power company was talking about the kids who've challenged Lakeland Construction to protect their science project!" Rachel tried to laugh, and a funny barking sound came out.

Hollis was painting a marsh wren with watercolors; he hadn't heard a word we'd said, not even Rachel's weird laugh. I was beginning to think that I was the only sane person in the cabin: I was the only one who understood that Wayburn's death sentence was already signed and that nothing could change it.

"Look," I said, "even Henry eventually left the woods. Mrs. Stark told us about that, remember? For him, the experiment wasn't over, it was just bigger even than the woods. He left because he wanted to explore other things."

"Don't lecture me about Thoreau!" Rachel shouted, finally getting Hollis's attention. "I know all about the last chapter of *Walden*. Thoreau stayed in the woods for two years and two months—we haven't had near that much time, and I'm not leaving until we do! I might not leave even then. Doesn't he say that everyone should march to his own music? Well, maybe my music is telling me to stay."

"But there will be nothing to stay *in*."

No one talked for a while, and the only sounds were the swish of Hollis's brush in a jar of water and the whistles of the song sparrows.

"Are you finished? Is that what you wanted to say?" Rachel asked.

"I guess so."

"Because I would like to talk about how we can *keep* Wayburn."

"Sounds good to me," Hollis said.

"Another plan, right?"

"That's right," Rachel said.

"And I suppose Stuart thought it up."

"Nope," she said. "This one is all mine."

Rachel's plan was to pick up where Stuart left off. His strategy was to pit the developers against the kids, right out in the open for the whole city to see. Rachel's idea was a sneak attack on the enemy itself. "We're going to pay a visit to Lakeland Construction and have a talk with them. They need to hear from us directly."

"The three of *us*?" I asked.

"Well, the two of you. I'm going to play a slightly different part," Rachel said. "I'll be there with you, of course, but I'll be going in the capacity of a school adviser . . . sort of a Mrs. Stark." Hollis and I stared speechlessly as Rachel went on.

"I know what you're thinking, but hear me out. The

Green Day Walkout is on Monday. Stuart has already warned the newspapers that something big is going to happen at school. After the walkout the entire city will be watching Lakeland Construction. They'll be backed into a corner, fearing more student revolts, more bad publicity. That's why it's critical that on Tuesday we visit their office in Meadowcreek Hills. We'll walk in calmly, ask to speak with the president, and give them an opportunity to gracefully back down from the project. You watch, they'll jump at the chance!"

I was having more than doubts about Rachel now. I was certain she was stumbling down some back alley in her mind and was headed for mental illness. I hoped that practicality might blast her back to common sense.

"We have no way to get there, no way to get back," I said.

"Phil can drive us," Hollis said, "before he goes to work."

"He'll just pull up to school in the Flying Devil and sign all of us out for . . . let's see . . . dentist appointments?" I said.

"No," she said, "we'll go after school. It would look odd if all three of us were absent on the same day. Time will be a problem, but we'll manage."

The student council was in high gear that week before the walkout. When the idea of the Green Day Convention was born, they probably believed it was their own invention. Yet who else but Stuart would have thought of inviting local government agencies like the Department of Forestry and the

Fish and Game Bureau to a convention at our school? And who else would have invited the Rare and Indigenous Plant Society and the North American Bird Conservancy to come too? And the press and politicians and environmental activists and anyone who might possibly have the slightest bit of interest in Wayburn Woods.

In the computer lab after school, student council representatives were churning out letters and making phone calls. School board members, municipal judges, city officials, radio and television stations—all received invitations to attend. Stuart even wrote a letter to Lakeland Construction, inviting them to join a discussion with young Americans entitled "How Best to Preserve our Natural Environment."

And like the Green Day Walkout, the Green Day Convention was top secret. Not one adult in the school knew that over two hundred special guests would be dropping by next week.

Early Saturday I went to Wayburn Woods. I got there after sunrise while fog still clung to the lake. It would probably be the last time that I'd see the forest whole. Already, Stephen had scouted out more changes. Men with tripods had been there all week, pointing instruments into the woods, throwing up invisible lines and barriers; they scribbled parcel numbers, recorded acreage. Hundreds of trees had been tagged with yellow ribbons for cutting.

I felt as if I were sitting up with a dying friend who didn't know she was dying. The squirrels were dashing in the undergrowth, rising on their haunches to peek at me. They hadn't seen the bulldozers yet, either. I went to the fern patch on the ridge above the cabin. For the last time I eased myself into the stillness and felt the forest growing up around me, breathing green and sweet through my lungs. Then I left and walked back on the original path that had led us to Wayburn so long ago.

Green Day was warm and bright. I reached the top step of the bus that morning and realized that with so much on my mind, I had forgotten to wear green clothes. On the one day I most needed to be camouflaged, I would stand out like an oddball.

Everyone was jittery at school, which was understandable since we had all left home that morning intending to take part in a premeditated crime. I guess that's why the social structure fell apart. Not that classroom behavior was bad. Actually, kids were trying hard to be *good* on Green Day. Yet when teachers turned toward chalkboards or grappled for items in cupboards, all of us urgently wanted to be assured that we would have plenty of company when we walked out at 1:15. It didn't matter that you had never spoken to the boy next to you in science, suddenly you were fellow mutineers. At lunch, the lines in the cafeteria were short; most kids were too uneasy to eat; they fidgeted with straws and saltshakers, their eyes on the clock.

I thought it was fateful that I was in Mrs. Stark's class when the Green Day Walkout began. Brendan Fain and Jake

Spenner were wrapped in white sheets, reading a scene from *Julius Caesar* at the front of the room. I also thought it interesting that Stuart was in class that day, not only because his attendance was so infrequent, but also because he would make such a good Julius Caesar.

The two stammering senators were the only ones reading the play because by then the countdown had begun. Larry, Chip, and Ben had flattened themselves against the backs of their chairs and were bracing for the liftoff signal like astronauts on a launchpad.

When the big hand finally came to rest on the quarter hour, however, we simply looked at each other. Nobody moved. Then we heard the tramping of feet, the nervous mumble of student voices, the shouts of teachers. All at once, three-fourths of Mrs. Stark's class stood up and headed for the door, hesitantly at first, each looking over his shoulder to be sure someone was following him. Mrs. Stark embraced her copy of *Julius Caesar* and closed her eyes.

"Stop! Stop right this minute and listen to me!" she called out. Ben Jones had reached the doorknob, but he stopped and listened one last time to Mrs. Stark. We all did.

"I know what you have planned for today, but I am obligated to inform you that if you walk out that door, you will be considered truant. The punishment for truancy is a two-day suspension from school, and you will not be able to make up missed work." Mrs. Stark waited while we considered these harsh realities.

"Students, this is what we call a *moral dilemma*," she said slowly, and the class groaned. The most exhilarating event of our lives was thundering past the door, and Mrs. Stark was turning it into a lesson. Ben's hand rattled the doorknob in warning.

"So weigh the consequences carefully"—she closed her eyes again—"and do what you must do."

Other classes had filed out of their rooms, but Mrs. Stark's group ruptured into the flow as though a dam had given way, causing the traffic to bottleneck above the stairs. Everyone rushed out of Room 23 except Rachel, Hollis, and me.

We were the last ones to exit through the front doors, so we had the rare sight of seeing the entire student body at the peak of its civil disobedience. Kids were circulating in large groups, and in the center of one I saw Janice Phelson's red hair flash with sunlight as she led the crowd in chanting "Wayburn! Wayburn!" Human pyramids rose up from the lawn. A few picket signs—SAVE THE FOREST, WAYBURN WOODS FOREVER—had been pulled out of the bushes and were held up by student council members. On the fringes of the crowd, some pushing and shoving broke out, but it was just horseplay, and overall, the Green Day Walkout was a pretty mild rebellion.

We stood by the hedges on the front walkway unnoticed until Larry Duncan came ambling by and saw Hollis.

"It's the bird boy!" Larry shouted. Larry and his friends lifted Hollis up on their shoulders and carried him through the crowd and up the slope to the sidewalk, where everyone could see him. The crowd parted before this parade, raising their voices in a salute: "Bird boy! Bird boy!"

Hollis was bounced and tossed and sometimes thrown so high he appeared to be airborne. But we never knew how high Hollis could have flown that day because suddenly Green Day came to a screeching halt. Half a dozen shiny black police cars pulled up on Pine Brook Drive, sirens blaring, lights flashing, and megaphones booming.

Chapter 18

"If you have built castles in the air, your work need
not be lost; that is where they should be.
Now put the foundations under them."
H. D. THOREAU

The photograph of Mr. Putterman that appeared in the
Detroit News the next morning wasn't flattering. The camera
had compressed his features into a frozen snarl and made his
heavy glasses look like the goggles of a gas mask. We all
knew about Mr. Putterman's military service and the dangers
he had faced as a tank commander in the Gulf War. He found
a way to weave his war stories into every school assembly.
And now on the front page of the newspaper, Mr. Putterman
was again at war.

Mr. Putterman filled the lower corner of the photo,
growling out an order to the arriving policemen. But the

photo had also captured Hollis just after the basketball team had tossed him up, so he seemed to be floating above Mr. Putterman's head. Hollis's arms were bent as if he were poised for flight, and he was gazing upward, with an expression so pure and intent he could have been on a Christmas card.

The caption read: "Schoolmates recognize Junior Audubon member Hollis Robbins for his commitment to wildlife conservation." I think the caption may have exaggerated the motives of the basketball team a bit. But the article below the photograph was no exaggeration. It gave all the details of the student protest that had taken place in front of Pine Brook School.

They called it a "massive demonstration." The article also accurately quoted Mr. Putterman's threat to call out the National Guard if students didn't return immediately to their classes. I'd heard that myself. Really, the photograph said it all. Anyone could see that Mr. Putterman, impatiently waving the police into position, had overreacted.

"I can't imagine students taking over a school like that," Mother said in the morning, the *Detroit News* spread out on the kitchen table.

"We didn't exactly take it over."

"You were involved in this, Beth?"

"Everyone was," I answered breezily. "We all left. It was like a school spirit day. The student council organized it. You sort of had to do it."

"Oh." Mother took another look at Mr. Putterman's

glowering face. "Well, maybe you ought to stay home today, in case more trouble breaks out."

"No, I have to go!" I said more desperately than I meant to. "Rachel and I are doing an assignment together. We have to do research at the library after school, so I'll probably be late, very late." I was stretching the truth on two counts, but I had no choice. I couldn't tell her that I was going to be involved in a more dangerous protest than the Green Day Walkout. How could I explain that we were going to the corporate offices of Lakeland Construction to bully them out of a housing development? My mother was far too fragile for that sort of information.

At school I was ordered to Mr. Putterman's office even before the final bell rang in homeroom. From the stares and blunt directions I received from the office staff, I realized how quickly your reputation can change. In less than a week my good citizenship record had been erased.

Mr. Putterman didn't seem to like his photograph in the *Detroit News* any more than I did, and he was tormenting himself with it when I walked into his office. He looked up from the newspaper clipping as I sat once again in the leather chair before his desk.

"I want to know what part you played in this," he said coldly.

"The picture?"

"The walkout!"

"I walked out like everyone else did, sir."

"Did you plan it?"

I looked into the round tunnels of his eyes. "No, I didn't plan it."

"Did you influence others to walk out of class to save your forest project?"

"No, I didn't influence anyone, I swear."

He studied me for a full minute. "I think," he said, rubbing his chin, "that you're more of a troublemaker than you look, and it's time we brought your parents in here to discuss just how involved you are. Mrs. Stemper!" he called over my head. "Mrs. Stemper, get me Elizabeth Gardner's phone number, please."

"Mr. Putterman, I haven't tried to cause any trouble, honestly."

"Miss Gardner, do you know what I think? I think you instigated that revolt yesterday, you and your radical friends, like this bird boy. What's more, I know you have something else planned. I want to know why I'm receiving RSVPs from city officials for a 'convention' here on Thursday. I want to know what the devil is going on!" he shouted.

Mrs. Stemper's heels tapped into the room and she handed him my phone number with obvious satisfaction.

"I only walked out like everyone else, Mr. Putterman. The difference is that I really cared about what we were doing."

He smiled sardonically. "Yes, I think that's the key issue, you care too much about this forest project, and in my opinion, you're becoming a detriment to this school!" Mr. Putterman picked up the receiver and began dialing my number. I went numb and felt an enormous weight pressing me into the chair. My arms were suddenly pinned to my sides. I could hardly breathe.

I saw our phone ringing at the other end of the line. Mother would be having a second cup of coffee; she always said those few hours before she went to the office were her favorite time of day. She would be humming, browsing in the paper. At first she wouldn't even understand who was calling. It would take a few minutes for her to connect the voice with the twisted face she had folded away and tucked under the fashion section of the newspaper. I waited for Mr. Putterman's voice to shoot off into the receiver like a machine gun, puncturing through the wall phone of our kitchen.

Then the door swung open and Stuart Garfield stepped into the principal's office, knocking lightly as he did so.

"Stuart, come back later, I'm busy," Mr. Putterman said, still dialing my number.

"Sir, I need to talk to you about the Green Day Walkout."

Mr. Putterman stopped dialing. "What do *you* know about it?"

"Everything. I should know everything, I planned it."

He hung up the phone, and I almost drooped over in relief that my mother would continue to sip her coffee, undisturbed and uninformed.

"Stuart, what are you telling me?" Mr. Putterman looked incredulous, as if he were watching a statue melt.

"That the walkout, the editorials in the paper, it was all

my idea. It was meant to get the attention of the whole community—a publicity stunt."

Mr. Putterman took off his glasses; he couldn't be hearing this correctly.

Stuart put his hand on the back of my chair. "Beth is innocent, Mr. Putterman. The only thing she's guilty of is following the example of a great American. And all we want to do is protect a forest. This protest isn't a mindless riot. It's a tribute to Henry David Thoreau, to the spirit of American independence and individuality."

What could Mr. Putterman say to that! Stuart pulled up an extra chair and sat down.

"Mr. Putterman, the Green Day Convention must go on."

"Nothing is going on until I know *exactly* what it is!"

So Stuart explained. He told Mr. Putterman that the Green Day Convention was supposed to be a surprise, that it was going to "unfold" right after the awards assembly while everyone was still in their seats. The mayor, retired judges, parents, "friends of nature"—they were all going to walk into our auditorium. There would be speeches and a final procession in which the homeroom representatives would carry the petitions up and present them to the mayor.

Mr. Putterman couldn't find anything to say to that, either. "But your role, sir, is the most important. Most principals would have canceled the Green Day Convention, afraid that students were getting out of hand, but not you. It will be your day, Mr. Putterman, and a great day for Pine Brook School."

I could see that Mr. Putterman liked Stuart's description of him as a patient, forgiving king, who in his great wisdom allowed his little subjects to speak their minds. When Stuart hinted that Mr. Putterman would have many chances to get another photo in the paper, he even joked, "Well, there's an idea, maybe I can get a decent picture out of this!"

The three of us stood up and Mr. Putterman inspected me in a new light. I was glad I had taken some extra pains with my appearance in anticipation of the visit to Lakeland Construction. He looked over my neatly flipped hair and my Glamma Girl skirt and blouse. Why, I didn't look like a dangerous radical at all! He gave me an awkward pat on the back and sent me back to class. I turned to Stuart as I walked out, wanting to say something about saving me from certain expulsion, but he and Mr. Putterman were already roughing out a written program for the Green Day Convention.

"Mrs. Stemper!" Mr. Putterman said. "We're going to need this typed up and copied by this afternoon."

Time is so unreliable. On the day I didn't want school to end, it galloped by me in a blur. Rachel was a nervous wreck and didn't look at all like herself. Her hair was clean and fluffy; her nails clipped, shaped, and even painted a deep coral. She wore the same old jeans and T-shirt in the same old messy way, but she kept alluding to the all-important satchel stored in her locker.

"Let's go over the sequence again," she said at lunch.

"Rachel, we've gone over it enough."

"First, we get the satchel and then you walk back with me to the girls' locker room," she said.

"Right."

"Then what?"

"Then Hollis meets his brother out front. I wait outside the P.E. door, watch for the Flying Devil, and flag them down."

"And then?"

"Then I wait ten minutes and meet you outside the locker room, carry the satchel with your regular clothes, and help you into the car."

"I won't need help, you'll just open the door and we'll both get in."

"All right," I said. "Then Phil drives us to Lakeland Construction in Meadowcreek Hills."

"Windward and Fifteenth Street."

"Yes." *And then we go off on an utterly pointless, hopeless trip,* I thought.

At the sound of the dismissal bell, the three of us fell into position, and for a while at least, everything went according to schedule. Hollis waited for Phil in front of the school, and Rachel and I carried the satchel to the girls' locker room so that she could begin some kind of magical identity change. The extracurricular sports programs were over for the year, and the locker room was certain to be deserted after the slowpokes from our class cleared out. I left Rachel sorting out the clothing in her satchel and laying it on the bench.

"You sure you don't want some help?"

"I'm positive. Now go and get to your post or you're going to throw off the whole plan." In her agitation she lifted out a crepe blouse carefully wrapped in tissue, unfolded it, and then folded it again. I was sure that Rachel had expertly planned her disguise, but I didn't see how she could change her appearance without a few tucks and pins from extra hands.

"Go! You're making me nervous," she said.

I stood outside and waited for Hollis and Phil. Right on time, I saw the frowning eyebrows of the Flying Devil pull slowly around into the side driveway and up to the sidewalk where I stood. Phil inclined his head slightly to show he was in place and ready. He looked just like a criminal in a getaway car; maybe I *was* sinking into a dark underworld and didn't even know it.

Now I had to fetch Rachel or whoever she had become and walk her to the car, and I would have, if not for the barrier that blocked my path. Cindy Wedford, Kathy Dulack, and a bunch of their friends had returned from the tennis courts and had flopped onto the floor outside the locker room in a sweaty, glamorous heap. Cindy's slender, tanned legs stretched out from beneath a tiny white pleated skirt. She kicked off her tennis shoes to better absorb the coolness of the tile floor, leaned her head languorously against the wall, and looked as though she intended to recuperate awhile.

Rachel would have to step over their sprawling bodies or wait for their inevitable move to the locker room. Either way, she was trapped.

I could see Hollis in the front seat, shrugging, telling Phil he had no idea what was taking so long. Phil was rapping his fingers slightly on the steering wheel. I decided that I would just get to the locker room and let Rachel choose her own route now that Cindy blocked the hallway.

Rachel evidently felt she had waited long enough and suddenly came out all by herself. At least I thought it was Rachel. The woman who stepped out wore a navy blue suit with a narrow skirt hitting just below her knees. She was con-servative, elegant, from the small wedge of cream-colored crepe at her neckline, and her string of pearls, to her navy-and-gray spectator pumps. Her hair was pulled into a neat chignon at the nape of her neck. Her only Rachel-like acces-sory was the black satchel, the one I was supposed to carry, which she now tossed irritably ahead of herself, down the hallway toward the resting tennis players. She fumbled in her purse for some item, all the while walking purposefully in her two-inch heels.

I couldn't be sure if Rachel didn't see the girls lying on the floor or if coming within inches of kicking their bare legs was part of her new personality. She finally found her brown tortoiseshell glasses in the bottom of her purse and slid them on. The world must have instantly sharpened into focus for Rachel, and at the same moment Cindy Wedford opened her hazy eyes and looked up. I think their mutual recognition was instantaneous.

"Excuse me," Rachel said, closing her purse with a snap, "if you ladies wouldn't mind." She was referring to their legs spread across the floor in rows of hurdles. The girls stared back, unable to grasp who was inside this prim costume.

"Your legs," Rachel said. "Please move them."

"Would you look at that. It's Rachel Haygen and she's all grown up!" Cindy looked Rachel's outfit over with a delighted smirk; here was an unexpected chance for fun!

"Do show us this new look you've got, Rachel. It's so . . . sophisticated. So . . . let's see, Mrs. Starkish." Cindy's eye for clothes was more astute than even she realized, for the outfit Rachel wore, down to the smallest accessory, *was* Mrs. Stark's. It was Mrs. Stark's first-day-of-school outfit and exactly what she would have worn if she had accompanied us to Lakeland Construction, had she not been afraid of jeopardizing her teaching position in the process.

"How will you ever climb into your tree fort in that? Aren't you afraid you'll ruin those shoes?" A master of sarcasm, Cindy had her friends giggling on cue. "And most important, how will you make your mud patties out there in the swamp?" The girls were already exhausted from four sets of tennis in the June sun, and all this hilarity was turning them punchy. They slapped playfully at Cindy to stop, then leaned against one another in helpless laughter.

"One other thing," Cindy squeaked, barely able to form

words between gasps for air, "we just have to know—those panty hose you're wearing—are they *control top* or *regular?*" More laughter followed.

Rachel listened impassively to Cindy's questions. She picked a piece of lint from the sleeve of her jacket, and then even from my position I could see a new expression dawning in her face. She was discovering the power of her gabardine suit and her string of pearls. If she could dress like Mrs. Stark, why couldn't she actually *be* Mrs. Stark? Maybe a suit of clothes could be a suit of armor. Maybe Rachel could be someone she had never been before.

"That's enough," she said. There was a moment's pause in the girls' hysterics.

"What did you say?" Cindy asked, dabbing tears from her eyes.

"I said, that's enough. I don't have time for this *nonsense.*" Something in the way Rachel said the word *nonsense* sent a chill through their damp bodies. They must have heard an old anger, long repressed and long overdue; I know I did.

"No time, huh?" Cindy continued. "Then maybe you had better get going. I do think I hear the squirrels calling you."

Rachel whirled around, leaned over, and put a well-manicured finger right under Cindy's nose. "And it's your nonsense I'm most tired of! Your rude, petty little nonsense! Now get out of my way!"

Cindy was so startled by the passion and authority

streaming out of Rachel that she shrank back, pallid and wide-eyed. Rachel had a number of hidden talents. One of them was the ability to throw objects low and fast; pillows, stuffed animals, even small bodies were tossed around the Haygen house with speed and precision. Rachel picked up the satchel, backed up about ten feet, and then sent it flying over the girls and down the length of the hallway. The tennis girls saw that black cannonball flying toward them and huddled down as low as they could. Kathy Dulack screamed and, fearing for her face, buried her head in Cindy's shoulder. Rachel buttoned her suit coat and smoothed back her hair. She placed the handle of her purse over her arm and said, "If you ladies wouldn't mind."

I'll never forget Rachel's walk to freedom. She didn't look back at the astounded faces, some still hidden behind tennis rackets. She walked head high, with practiced ease in those grown-up clothes. When she finally reached me, I opened the door, took the satchel, and escorted her to the Flying Devil, just like she'd planned.

Chapter 19

"The universe is wider than our views of it."
H. D. THOREAU

The backseat of Phil's car was like a time capsule of his life. We climbed in over candy bar wrappers, empty soda cans, cast-off work shirts from the Drexter factory, a gas can, and jars of motor oil.

He was cheerful, though, for an older brother who was chauffeuring a bunch of ninth graders around town on his night off. I thought he was probably enjoying the mood of this errand; we had stepped into his creepy world, and he seemed delighted to be showing us around.

"All right, Phil," Rachel said, fastening her seat belt. "We have a four o'clock appointment at Lakeland Construction. Can you make it?"

Phil caught her eyes in his rearview mirror. "If that's what you want, Miss Schoolteacher, you got it. I might have to break a few rules, though."

The Flying Devil backed out of the parking space slowly enough, and Phil drove calmly up Pine Brook Drive. Rachel straightened her clothing and read some note cards she'd pulled from her purse.

"Not a speech, exactly," she explained, "just some ideas in case Lakeland Construction needs a little coaxing."

I didn't say anything. I would leave this whole scheme to Rachel. If her navy blue suit could conquer Cindy Wedford, then who could say? Maybe she could intimidate a multimillion-dollar construction company. But it seemed unlikely. From a distance she had appeared tailored and impeccable, but at close range her image wasn't as credible. Stray hairs were escaping her chignon, the ends of her elegant blouse were dangling from under her jacket, her collar was askew, and nervous perspiration was shining on her nose. "Mrs. Stark" was slowly unraveling, and the fourteen-year-old girl underneath was showing through.

When the Flying Devil turned onto Windward Avenue, it suddenly surged forward, springing into the evening traffic. Phil had the car in fourth gear in a matter of seconds and began a game of lane changing that was like an insanely fast round of checkers. Rachel and I were tossed and slammed about in the tumble of junk in the backseat. Phil was maneuvering shrewdly through the stream of cars, laughing every time I gasped at our near collisions.

"My mother thinks we're at the library," I said to Rachel in between lurches. "The library! Think how surprised she'll be when I call from the police station or maybe the hospital!"

"Relax. We're almost there and we're going to be on time. Thank goodness for that. Tardiness wouldn't look good at all. Five minutes could have cost us all of Wayburn Woods."

Hollis and I waited outside the sleek wooden building that housed Lakeland Construction while Rachel touched up her lipstick and fixed her hair. Before we reached the front doors, she stopped us with last-minute instructions.

"I'll do all the introductions and the explanations as to why we're here. Follow my cues. If I think one of you should speak, then I'll say so; otherwise, don't go blabbing out any-thing." We listened and nodded. Rachel looked the building over as though it were an enemy fort.

"I may *look* like Mrs. Stark, but I'll be calling myself Mrs. Emerson—she was a friend of Thoreau's—so whatever you do, don't call me Rachel!"

The entry to Lakeland Construction was lush with azaleas and Japanese maples. Beside the small patio was a pebble-lined pond thick with water plants and koi. The headquarters of the evil developers was not at all what I thought it would be. I had expected an ugly building on some bleak, dead wasteland, but Lakeland Homes, as the discreet sign read, was pretty nice. We followed Rachel into the vestibule, where our feet sank into the carpet and our eyes adjusted to the dim, cool interior. When the door slid shut, the traffic sounds from Windward Avenue were replaced by the trickling of water.

"Look at that!" Hollis exclaimed. "It's a heron!" Actually three herons, cast in bronze, stood wading in a corner. Water splashed over them from an invisible source and gathered in a green pool at their feet. Rachel glared at him; he had already broken the first rule.

"Sorry," he whispered, and clapped his hand over his mouth.

"Good afternoon. May I help you?" a pleasant voice came from behind a reception desk in a lamplit corner. "Do you have an appointment?" The voice slowly became a female face framed by oak paneling and ferns.

"Yes, we have an appointment," Rachel replied a little defensively. "I'm Mrs. Emerson, and these are students from Pine Brook School. We've come about the building project in Wayburn Woods." Rachel walked up to the voice's desk, but Hollis and I hung back, trying to look younger than Mrs. Emerson.

"With whom is your appointment?" the woman asked.

"With Mr. Giles, of course. I should think you would have a record of it. I made the appointment last week!" Rachel's voice was shrill and edgy; this was not the controlled, adult impression that she had hoped to make, but the well-trained voice behind the desk gave no hint that anything was wrong.

"Mrs. Emerson, I'm terribly sorry"—the voice hesitated for a split second as the receptionist scanned a notebook—"but Mr. Giles was detained at a meeting and regrets that he will not be able to meet with you and the students today."

"What? Do you realize the trouble we've gone to—we even got here on *time*!"

"I am sorry, Mrs. Emerson. We did try to notify you this afternoon; however, the phone number you gave us was no longer in use, so we couldn't reach you. Perhaps you'd like to reschedule for sometime next week?"

Rachel looked angry and embarrassed. "Next week will be too late. By then these children will be out of school and the opportunity to participate in a . . . conservation project will be lost forever. I just can't let them down!" Hollis and I were actually relieved that the vice president wasn't there, but we did our best to look disappointed.

The telephone on the voice's desk was lighting up with incoming calls. "There's nothing I can do, Mrs. Emerson. Mr. Giles will not be returning to the office today, but the students are welcome to go in and see the model home display for Wayburn Manor Estates."

"No, that won't be enough. They don't need to see models. They need to see a developer. It's part of their project—an interview with a real person." Rachel wasn't talking to the voice anymore, but to the tops of her spectator pumps, half-buried in the thick rug. She was no longer clutching her purse in that self-assured way; now it dangled from her fingertips. She was deflating right in front of us and was in danger of jeopardizing her disguise. I should have let the plan die then and there, but instead I spoke up without permission.

"Mrs. Emerson, we'd like to see those models. They might be really interesting and helpful to our project." I looked encouragingly at our defeated teacher. "Don't you think so too, Hollis?"

"Sure, you bet. I always like to see models."

Mrs. Emerson couldn't muster much enthusiasm for the model homes, but the voice seemed glad to get rid of us and directed us down the hall to the conference room where Wayburn Manor Estates was on display for a board meeting. She even pointed out the back door, so that after we had seen the exhibit we could leave more conveniently.

"I'll be closing up the office in about ten minutes. I hope that will give you plenty of time for your research."

A long table and chairs dominated the conference room. At the far end was a kitchenette and another table displaying architectural drawings. The exterior wall was solid glass and looked out into a courtyard of begonias and flowering crab-apple trees. In the center of the room up against the window was a covered platform about the size of the Haygens' Ping-Pong table, and on it, Wayburn Woods was stretched out and sealed in a Plexiglas coffin.

"That's Wayburn Lake!" Hollis said. "And Middleton Road, but . . ." But that was all we recognized. The forest that surrounded the lake had been replaced with hundreds and hundreds of little roofs and the geometric pattern of their lawns. Lakeland Construction was so far ahead of us. They already knew the design of every house. They had even laid out the curve of each driveway and stenciled in the names of the streets.

"The houses are all over the place! I thought you said they sold off only part of the forest. I thought the birds could spread out across the lake, but here, there's no place for them to go!" Hollis's voice cracked.

Rachel pointed to a small placard near the three-tiered hill that said Phase 2. Then she searched around the lake until she found Phase 3. It was in Mr. Wayburn's pastures where the dairy cattle grazed.

"They do it in stages," I said. "It'll take years to build this. I don't think even Mr. McDuff knows it's going to be this big—but then, maybe he does."

We heard the whoosh of the receptionist's skirt and the click of light switches in the hallway.

"Mrs. Emerson?" the voice called. Rachel turned to the door but didn't answer. "Mrs. Emerson? Are you still here?" Hollis and I threw urgent looks at Rachel, but she still didn't answer. The clicking of more switches and the swish of a light raincoat brought the voice even closer.

Without a warning Rachel ran to the table at the back of the room, bent down, and crawled under it. The last thing I saw were her high-heeled feet vanishing behind the model home layouts. Hollis and I had no choice but to follow her. How would we have explained the disappearance of our teacher? I crawled into the darkness beside Rachel. Hollis hugged his legs to his chest and leaned into us to avoid the shaft of light coming in from the only unblocked side of the table.

"Mrs. Emerson?" The voice trailed off when she saw that the conference room was empty. She straightened a few chairs and then did a terrifying thing: she walked to our side of the room and stood at the window. Hollis could see her feet and leaned back so far that he rolled into our laps. Rachel, wedged against the wall, was laboring against her tailored suit, holding her breath to keep the taffeta lining from rustling. Her tense face was inches from mine. We listened as the receptionist drew the draperies across the windows. She then went into the kitchenette, rinsed out a coffeepot, wiped a counter, and studied for long, tortured moments the contents of the mini refrigerator. Suddenly she whisked past us again, then turned off the light that striped our cubbyhole and was gone. We sat in the dark for some time before anyone spoke.

"What are we doing here?" I finally asked.

"I needed more time to think," Rachel said.

"If we get caught, they'll call this breaking and entering!"

"We're not going to break anything, and as far as entering, they invited us in. We just haven't left yet. There's no law against that!" Rachel whispered hotly.

"I guess it's safe to turn on the lights," Hollis said. He crawled across the room, feeling his way around the conference chairs and the display case until he found the opposite wall and the overhead light switch. Rachel and I squirmed out and stood before Wayburn Manor Estates with its tiny fake trees and shrubbery. I was shivering, even though it was a warm spring evening.

"What about Phil? What will he do if we stay in here too long?" I asked.

Hollis shrugged. "Nothing much. Probably get a burger or something. I'll go tell him to wait."

"No! Don't go out the door!" Rachel said. "You might set off an alarm. See if you can find a window that opens onto the parking lot. Signal him from there. Tell him . . . we'll need as much time as he can give us. The library closes at eight, so we have to leave by then."

"Eight o'clock! What will we do all that time?" I asked.

"We're going to leave a message for Lakeland Construction." Rachel nodded at the Wayburn display. "They left us one, now it's our turn to reply."

"And the alarm? What will happen when we do leave? We'll set it off!"

"Yes, but then . . . we'll have the Flying Devil." Rachel took off her jacket, rolled up the sleeves of her blouse, and kicked off her high heels. "Come on, we need some materials."

We took a few sheets of typing paper and some pencils from the top of the receptionist's desk. I refused to open the drawer. "Remember, Rachel. We hurt nothing, break nothing, and everything goes back in its place. That's what Henry would do."

"Fine. Although I don't see why you're being so careful

with people who are about to hack down a forest." She paced around the model home display. "We should smash all those little houses or, better yet, steal them and leave the whole board empty—take down the street signs and leave only the trees. If we could get it out the door, it could be strapped to the roof of the Flying Devil and we could drive it to Wayburn, set it on fire, and then push it into the lake."

"Why not just wait and see what Stuart can do at the Green Day Convention?" I suggested.

"Do you think I believed for one second that Stuart could save Wayburn with one of his speeches? I'm going to get more paper."

Hollis sat at the conference table, doing what he always did when left on his own. He drew. Rachel and I sat with him and argued about the message we would leave. One promising idea was to collect leaves from the courtyard and toss them all over the display case, over the whole room. But that would mean opening the outside door and setting off the alarm.

Another was to write a long letter, using only one word per page, and hang it on the walls. We considered typing a letter on the receptionist's computer, so it would be the first thing they saw in the morning. Every idea eventually seemed silly and futile when we thought of the bulldozers parked above the Old Grove. We were getting nowhere, and it was almost dark outside.

"The cover has to go," Rachel said. "I can't think when I'm staring into that case."

Lifting the Plexiglas lid off Wayburn wasn't easy. It

was heavy and awkward, and we discovered that there was no place to set it except up against the kitchenette. Rachel's corner slipped and broke some plastic trees on the north side of the lake, not far from the spot where we'd planned to begin our great summer expedition.

"Oh well, what's a tree or two?" she said. "I'm sure that's Lakeland's motto." Once it was off, we could reach in to trace the profile of the shoreline and pinpoint the sites we knew so well. The three-tiered hill had been smoothed out and a road called Mourning Dove Drive ran down its middle. It splayed out into side streets: Woodpecker Lane, Bluebird Way, and Robin Court. We found the inlet where Rachel picked cattails and from there estimated the location of the Old Grove. Hollis leafed through his drawings and placed a sketch of a great horned owl on the spot. The bird was rising up from its nest in the hollow of the oak, ruffled and apprehensive, as if intruders had been sighted.

"Of course!" Rachel shouted. "The birds! Hollis, your birds will leave the message for Lakeland. No one has more right to speak than they do."

"How many sketches have you got?" I asked.

"Five, six maybe. They're mostly sparrows."

"We need more . . . flickers, redwings, wrens, finches. Get busy!"

Hollis bent over the papers and dashed off portraits. I recalled how stiff and childlike his early sketches had been, but now from a few strokes of his pencil, lively birds sprang off the page. They preened and cocked their heads, flicked their tails and puffed out their feathers. Hollis told us where to place them on the display: the robin would go in the open country north of the hills, the red-headed woodpecker in the birches near the cabin, the wood duck in the inlet. He gave us page after page, and we didn't stop until we'd smothered every plastic house. Then we put the clear lid back in place and Hollis's birds were sealed in.

"Do you remember that first time we met in Stark's class?" Rachel asked him. "You wanted to make a model of Walden Pond out of papier-mâché, and I gave you a really hard time."

Hollis smiled. "You always give me a hard time."

"Well, I thought it was time I told you: I'm glad you joined our group that day."

This time Hollis laughed. "And I'm really glad you didn't let me make that model!"

The Flying Devil was idling in the parking lot at exactly eight o'clock. As Hollis and Rachel ran out the back door, I returned to the conference room to flick off the lights. I stood in the doorway a moment, knowing we'd wasted our time. Ten thousand bird sketches wouldn't stop those bulldozers. Tomorrow they'd flex and stretch their steel muscles and claw their way to the forest again. Even the Green Day Convention would come too late. I didn't voice my dark predictions once we were in the Flying Devil. Besides, Hollis and Rachel were listening for the security alarm, which, to their great disappointment, never went off.

Chapter 20

"In wilderness is the preservation of the world."
H. D. THOREAU

Sometime during the night I made a decision. I was going to live out the summer in the cabin, maybe the rest of my life. They wouldn't bulldoze over a person. They might try to blast me out with dynamite or tear down the cabin walls, but even that wouldn't stop me. I'd tunnel underneath the floorboards and live like a troll in a damp but cozy cave. Or I could live in a tree if I had to. Hollis could help me build a platform high in the white oaks, with ladders and a thatched roof. Or I could build a raft out of fallen logs and live on the lake like Huckleberry Finn. These things weren't impossible. Somebody had to take a stand in Wayburn Woods, and it was going to be me.

I stuffed my backpack with supplies and made sandwiches for lunch and dinner; beyond that I'd rely on Rachel and the forest for food. I rolled knives, tools, matches, and soap into my sleeping bag and strapped the bundle to my handlebars. I had no intention of going to school that day or maybe ever again. They wouldn't miss me at the Green Day Convention; besides, I had more important things to do than listen to speeches.

Mother wasn't awake yet when I looked in at her from the hallway. It wasn't quite five o'clock, and it didn't seem like a good time to tell her I was moving into the forest. I'd have to break it to her slowly over the next few days. I pulled my bike from the garage and walked it quietly up the driveway.

I crossed Middleton before I reached Rachel's house so that none of the Haygens could see me from an upstairs window as I slipped into the trees. The bulldozers were still sleeping when I crept past them, down to the meadow and across the three-tiered hill. I stashed my bike in the birch grove and carried all that I owned in one big armful.

Now the real experiment would begin. I would live alone in the woods, keeping a journal and bathing in the lake. I would befriend foxes and muskrats. I would dig a root cellar and store food for the winter, and on frigid nights I would lie in the cabin and hear the unearthly moan of expanding ice. Tadpoles in the inlet would grow to adulthood, and I would be the only one to see. I would become a hermit girl who patrolled the woods and kept the bulldozers and houses away.

Above the door of the cabin, Rachel had hung bunches of pennyroyal, her way of warning off intruders. I moved the furniture to make a sleeping area, swept the floor, and unpacked my supplies. Then I gathered kindling and wood for the stove. I brought a bucket of fresh water from the lake, washed the cabin window, and then sat down in the doorway and ate all three of my sandwiches. I'd have to forage for dinner.

The bulldozers came alive about seven o'clock, though their rumbling remained distant, as if they were tearing up more ground along Middleton. I puttered around the cabin and the woodpile to keep myself from feeling the strangeness of being alone. *Walden* lay open on the table, and seeing it there reminded me that I wasn't actually by myself. I still had Henry to talk to. I searched the beginning chapters for the famous quote Mrs. Stark had shown us back in the fall. I read it, and as usual, she'd left out the best part:

I wanted to live deep and suck out all the marrow of life, to live so sturdily and Spartan-like as to put to rout all that was not life, to cut a broad swath and shave close, to drive life into a corner, and reduce it to its lowest terms . . .

She had probably thought the class wouldn't understand it. But I knew what Henry was getting at, and the quote was like cold water splashed in my face. I wanted to drive life into a corner too, but unless I got busy saving the forest, there weren't going to be any corners left.

So with my pocketknife, I cut off all the yellow ribbons

on the trees in the Old Grove. I grabbed survey stakes and pulled them from the ground, stuffing them into my backpack. By the day's end I was going to rescue every tree west of the three-tiered hill. There was no turning back now. I had stepped over the line and had become a criminal. Too bad Mr. Putterman couldn't see me now. He had been right all along: I was more of a troublemaker than even he suspected.

I was returning to the cabin, hungry and exhausted, when Rachel came running down the path, still carrying her schoolbooks. "I knew it!" she shouted from the birches. "I knew you had to be here!"

She jogged up to the clearing, breathing hard. She took in the yellow ribbons spilling out of my pockets, my dirty hands and clothes, the survey flags bulging from my backpack.

"What have you done?" she asked incredulously.

"What we said we'd do. I'm saving Wayburn Woods. By tomorrow I'll have the ribbons off every tree—but those survey markers, they're going to take longer. They're spread all over the place and in no particular pattern."

While I emptied my pockets of ribbon, Rachel was strangely quiet. She opened the cabin door cautiously and peered inside as if she was afraid she'd disturb something.

"Are you going to sleep here?" she asked.

"I'm going to live here, Rache. I'm going to be Henry. Say, do you think Mrs. Stark would give me extra credit for starting up a new experiment?"

She didn't even smile.

"There are only two days of school left," I continued.

"It's not like I'm going to miss much, right? But I'm going to need your help with food until then. You'll help me, won't you? With those swamp potatoes and cattail parts?"

"This isn't a good idea, Beth. What will happen if the bulldozers come down into the Old Grove? They may not know you're here and—"

"I'll make sure they know. They won't plow me under, if that's what you're worried about. They just won't." Interestingly, that was the first time Rachel had admitted that bulldozers even existed. She must have known as I did that the bird sketches we left on the model homes were hopeless.

"What does your mom say about your living here?" she asked.

"She doesn't know yet," I said, glancing at my watch. That ordeal was still two hours away, when I estimated Mother would be home from work.

Rachel stared at me, as if she couldn't believe how reckless I'd become. "When you come back to school, they'll give you a detention for an unexcused absence."

"Rachel," I said steadily, "I'm not *going* back."

Hollis came meandering down the path about that time, and thankfully, he wasn't as shocked by my truancy as Rachel was.

"Hey, this is very heroic of you," he said. "Next week we can all move out here. I'll set up a pup tent over there by the fire ring and you ladies can have the cabin."

Rachel looked sadly at the ground, and suddenly I knew what was bothering her. She couldn't move into the forest, now or ever. For all her tough talk, Rachel wasn't really a rebel. Those Perfect Behavior Certificates she'd earned every year in school weren't for nothing. At heart she was a responsible, law-abiding, good citizen. I had turned out to be the rebel.

"You know, it doesn't matter who stays in the cabin," I said, "as long as somebody protects the forest, that's all that matters."

She nodded, but I could see she bitterly wished she could join me.

They left early, and I think it was all my stuff lying around that made them uncomfortable. Rachel didn't cook up any snacks, and that disappointed me, for I was starving. I walked with them to the three-tiered hill and watched them cross the meadow before I headed back to the cabin.

Truthfully, I was dreading the next few hours, when Mother would realize I was missing. That discovery loomed ahead like a ticking bomb, and I wasn't sure I was courageous enough to let it explode. I found a cup of dehydrated soup in Rachel's pantry and lit a small fire. After about ten minutes, the water still hadn't boiled. I had just stuck my finger in the kettle to see if it was warm, when someone knocked on the cabin door.

I sat by the stove, terror-stricken. Lakeland Construction had come to investigate the bird pictures. They were looking for the *vandals* who had lifted up the plastic lid and broken the plastic trees. My heart was racing. And then a horrific thought—the survey markers and yellow tape were right outside the cabin! By ripping up those survey markers, I'd ruined weeks and weeks of their work and then had led them to me. Why had we never put a lock on the door!

When I swung the door open, I saw Mr. McDuff in the clearing. "You didn't exaggerate about this grove of trees," he said. "It's extraordinary." He turned to the lake. "And that view!" he marveled, shaking his head. "It's worth a million bucks, and I don't say that lightly."

Wouldn't you know, the first thing he'd think about was money. I admit that I was ready to forgive him, though, when I saw that he was carrying a Blitz bag.

"How did you find me?" I asked.

"I had some idea where the cabin was, and when I passed your friends on the trail they gave me more detailed directions."

"But how did you know I'd be here?"

"Isn't this where you go every day after school?"

"Yes—but today I didn't go to school."

"I know. I stopped by your house this afternoon and intercepted a call from Mrs. Stemper, the attendance clerk. She was calling to verify your absence."

Would I ever be free of the high-minded Mrs. Stemper, or would she stalk me all my life?

"May I come in?" Mr. McDuff asked.

"Oh, sure!" I kicked my sleeping bag out of the way and pushed the card table against the wall.

"We built it to look like Henry's cabin, the one in *Walden*," I said, as he gave it the McDuff Realty walk-through, though there wasn't anywhere to walk.

"Quite a snug little house." He tapped the wall for soundness. "How long are you planning to stay?" he asked.

"As long as it takes. I'm going to stop them from building Wayburn Manor Estates."

"I see."

"I got the idea last night. If I'm living here, they won't be able to cut down the old trees or crush the cabin. If I can hold out long enough, maybe they'll change their minds and call the bulldozers off."

I expected him to start talking slowly, soothingly, like they do to crazy people, but instead he nodded respectfully. "Well, honey, is there any way I can help? Do you need anything?"

"No, I'll be fine. I've got extra clothes, and Rachel can get me food."

He set the Blitz bag on the card table. "Here's some dinner if you get hungry." He looked frustrated, and I sensed he wanted to do more for me. He had done more than he realized. I appreciated his calmness, his understanding, his willingness to walk all the way out here in his suit just to bring me dinner.

"I could use your help with one thing," I began. "Mother won't like it at all that I'm out here, and if she knew that I was trying to stop bulldozers—"

"Don't worry about your mother. I can cover you for one night, but beyond that I can't promise anything."

"Thank you, Louis." I was planning on trying out a new name for Mr. McDuff after the wedding, but now seemed like

237

the right time to start. He seemed pleased and before he left he scribbled a note of excuse for Mrs. Stemper, in case I ever went back to school, alluding to "Miss Gardner's legal affairs."

I didn't do anything spectacular on my one night as a resident of Wayburn Woods. I spent the evening as Henry would have, reading, writing in my journal; except I had the added bonus of a cheeseburger and chocolate shake.

The last chapter of *Walden* is not as sad as I thought it would be. I read it by candlelight while frogs chirped outside the cabin. Henry doesn't talk much about leaving the woods; mostly he gives a lot of advice, as if he's trying to squeeze in all that he learned from *his* Experiment in Living. My favorite was the story of a bug that hatched inside an old table after sixty years and then chewed its way through the wood to freedom. I was eager to tell Hollis about what surely had to be the most heroic bug of all time. Henry ends *Walden* by saying we all have a "beautiful and winged life" inside us too, and that it may gnaw its way out under the right conditions.

When I woke, the cabin was warm and flooded with sunlight. All I could find in the pantry were some squishy graham crackers and raisins for breakfast. I searched the corners of my backpack for a forgotten candy bar but found only a square of folded paper. Brittle and yellowed, it crackled when I opened it, like those fake copies of the Declaration of Independence you can buy at museum gift shops. The ink from Stuart's calligraphy pen had run a bit, but the lettering at the top of the page was unmistakable: THE HENRY CONTRACT.

How strange to read it after all this time and to see how carefully Stuart had listed the foods we would eat, the rules we would follow. I tucked it in the pocket of my jeans and put on my empty backpack so that I could fill it up with another load of tree tape and survey stakes. I traversed the meadow, but instead of taking the path toward Middleton, I headed north to the unexplored woods beyond. With every step the Henry Contract rustled in my pocket.

After cutting a couple of dozen tree ribbons, I impulsively pulled it out and read it again, curious to see if there was an ending date. There wasn't. Stuart had written only the beginning date and place for our Experiment in Living. I stopped and closed my pocketknife. An idea was chomping in my mind to get out, just like that bug buried deep in the old table. Wasn't there something sacred about contracts? We'd made a contract to live like Henry David Thoreau; it said so right there on the paper. They couldn't just barge in and throw us out. Wayburn Woods was part of that contract!

I was on fire with ideas. We could publish the Henry Contract in the *Detroit News*. We could get a lawyer and take our case to court—all the way to the Supreme Court. The Green Day Convention was going to begin at one o'clock, which left me an hour to ride my bike about eight miles and find Stuart before the program began.

I left my backpack in the woods and ran to the birch grove, scrambling up the path with my bike. I hit the pavement on Middleton and then really took off, flying along the curves that bordered Hawthorn Lake. After the intersection at Crestview Drive I was forced onto the shoulder by the heavy traffic, until I finally turned into Pine Brook Drive.

The driveway and parking lot were a logjam of cars. Were all these people here for the Green Day Convention? No, end-of-the-year awards were being presented first this afternoon—parents always flocked to that assembly. I squeezed my way up to the front door and leaned my bike against the hedge. Judging by the deserted hallways, they'd already started. The office was a ghost town. Even the dedicated Mrs. Stemper was missing from the attendance window. The patter of frantic feet echoed down a hall. A band member in full marching dress was buttoning up his coat with one hand and carrying his trumpet in the other.

"Where is everyone?" I asked.

"The auditorium," he said, trotting past me.

I followed him. "For the awards assembly?"

"Cancelled! The governor's here! It's that forest convention—the whole *city's* here!" He broke into a run and disappeared.

The *governor!* Stuart said the governor had the power to *pardon* Wayburn Woods, free it from death row. I dashed down two flights of stairs, passing up the trumpet player.

At the entry to the auditorium, I was nearly knocked off my feet by the roar. I backed up against the lockers to let a news crew pass with television cameras whirring on their shoulders. On the stage, Governor Wilson was shaking hands with a beaming Mr. Putterman. Light bulbs flashed. The crowd in the bleachers blared words so loud and shrill, they were unintelligible. I edged into the mob at the doorway to look for Hollis and Rachel, but the student section was packed so tightly I couldn't tell one face from another. The cheerleading squad was waving leafy branches as pom-poms, shouting, "Victory, victory to Wayburn Woods!" The student council had covered every wall with painted trees, with tall, straight trunks and round green tops—the way little kids draw. But they looked beautiful to me.

I stepped behind the open door, peering through the glass window at the elderly ladies from the Rare and Indigenous Plant Society as they stepped timidly into the commotion. Mr. Mitchell ushered in representatives from the Audubon Society and seated them in the front row. Countless adults filled the chairs across the basketball courts. I remembered the spring thaw in Wayburn Woods, how water had seeped out of every part of the forest and trickled down to the lake. A similar thaw was happening here; all of us who loved the woods were merging into one enormous pool that lapped the walls of the auditorium and spilled out the doorways. I retreated into the shadow of my hiding place because suddenly I couldn't swallow and my eyes blurred with tears. Stuart had done it. He had whipped a school's conscience into action.

The cheering from the bleachers began to die out and a restless murmur replaced it. A few taps of a baton brought the band to life. They slid into the first uncertain notes of "America the Beautiful."

Then I spotted Stuart. He was pacing, watching the staircase, as if he was expecting someone. He wore a tie, sport coat, and dress slacks. Stuart may have looked like the rest of us, but sometimes I suspected he was a different species altogether. He came from the same rootstock as Mr. McDuff. They both had the same hard-driving energy and ambition that built shopping malls and space stations. But Henry, like a log in a stream, had altered Stuart's course, probably forever. Stuart would be a new kind of industrialist; he would guard instead of conquer, respect instead of ravage.

I walked out to meet him and he rushed toward me, exasperated. "Where've you been? I've been looking for you since yesterday!"

Stuart may have organized this rally down to the smallest detail and snared the governor, but I hadn't exactly been idle. There wasn't time, though, to tell him about our raid on the Lakeland office or my plan to challenge the bulldozers. I didn't even pull the Henry Contract out of my pocket.

"I've been trying to find a way to save the woods," I said, looking into his strained face. "Because I didn't believe your convention could make a difference. But *look* at the people you've brought—the governor, the mayor—it's miraculous!"

"No. There's no miracle. The governor couldn't save Wayburn after all. He's here today to commend our civic spirit." Stuart couldn't hide his disappointment. "But the developers are getting pressured by environmental groups—the wildlife conservationists, the Audubon people, Rachel's rare plant society—to stop the building project. The state is going to send scientists to Wayburn, to confirm that it's an old growth forest. That way they can turn it into a preserve. Mr. Mitchell says the case will end up in the courts and will take years to settle. I know we'll win though, eventually."

A *preserve*. I wasn't sure I liked that idea. Wayburn Woods wouldn't be ours any more. But had it ever been? The forest was a living, breathing creature—immense, magnificent— with a life of its own and a right to exist on its own. And it would take all of our gifts combined to protect it.

Stuart looked at his watch uneasily and put a program into my hands. "I'm sorry to surprise you with this—I know it's short notice—but, there's something I need you to do—"

I saw with growing alarm that I was listed in the program as a speaker, the *first* speaker. I handed it back. "You're the one who gives speeches Stuart, not *me*!"

The band members had never had a larger or more supportive audience. They were approaching the final chorus of "America" with nearly reckless abandon.

"Just *talk* to them" Stuart said, "the way you do every week in the *Press*. Your column, Beth, your life in the woods—it was always the best part of the paper, and it brought out the best in us."

The band struck the last note. I was struck wordless at the thought of walking into that thronging room. But, under the shelter of Wayburn's trees, I had grown immeasurably, and it was time to step out of the shade.

Stuart led me to the door. "Mr. Putterman will announce you and then you'll go to the podium." He put his hand on my shoulder. "There it is, your introduction!" My name reverberated down from the heights of the auditorium. Stuart gave me a little push, and as a canoe slides out from the shore, I drifted into an ocean of people.

I headed in what I hoped was the direction of the podium, but I had lost all my bearings. Thousands of faces greeted me, guided me forward. I saw them applauding, yet I heard no sound. Kids waved from the bleachers, their mouths open, but I heard nothing. There was only a soft, distant roar that could have been wind blowing through the Old Grove, or rain on the cabin roof. I found Hollis and Rachel easily now; in fact, in this frenzied silence I could find any face I chose, and suddenly I had a lot to say.

For us there would be a summer with no end, and trails to the world's green edges, long nights of cricket song. Through all of us, Wayburn was spreading, sending out roots and vines, uniting with all the forests in the world. For Henry, the path back to *Walden* would be forever safe. I found the microphone and was no longer afraid. I would take them with me to the forest, to see the shadow under the fern, the sun on the treetops.

ROBIN VAUPEL has always been fascinated by the life of Henry David Thoreau and his experiment at Walden Pond. Her belief that young people have much to gain from Thoreau's acquaintance inspired this story. This is her first novel. She lives in California, where she is an award-winning teacher of eighth-grade literature.